FLINT SPEARS

Flint Spears

FLINT SPEARS

Cowboy Rodeo Contestant

By
WILL JAMES

Illustrated with drawings by the author

Mountain Press Publishing Company
Missoula, Montana
2002

First Printing, February 2002

*Tumbleweed is a registered trademark of
Mountain Press Publishing Company*

Library of Congress Cataloging-in-Publication Data

James, Will, 1892–1942.
Flint Spears : cowboy rodeo contestant / by Will James ;
illustrated with drawings by the author.
   p. cm. — (Tumbleweed series)
   ISBN 0-87842-449-0 — ISBN 0-87842-450-4
   1. Rodeo performers—Fiction 2. Cowboys—Fiction.
3. Rodeos—Fiction.   I. Title.
   PS3519.A5298 F56 2002
   813'.52—dc21
                                        2001008290

PRINTED IN THE UNITED STATES OF AMERICA

Mountain Press Publishing Company
P.O. Box 2399 • Missoula, Montana 59806
(406) 728-1900

PUBLISHER'S NOTE

WILL JAMES'S BOOKS are an American treasure. His writing and drawings captivated generations of readers with the lifestyle and spirit of the American cowboy and the West. Following James's death in 1942, the reputation of this remarkable writer and artist languished, and nearly all of his twenty-four books went out of print. But in recent years, publication of several biographies and film documentaries on James, public exhibitions of his art, and the formation of the Will James Society have renewed interest in his work.

Now, in conjunction with the Will James Art Company, Mountain Press is reprinting all Will James's books under the name the Tumbleweed Series, taking special care to keep each volume faithful to the original. Books in the Tumbleweed Series contain all the original artwork and text, feature an attractive new design, and are printed on acid-free paper.

The republication of Will James's books would not have been possible without the help and support of the many fans of Will James. Because all James's books and artwork remain under copyright protection, the Will James Art Company has been instrumental in providing the necessary permissions and furnishing artwork.

The Will James Society was formed in 1992 as a nonprofit organization dedicated to preserving the memory and works of Will James. The society is one of the primary catalysts behind a growing interest not only in Will James and his work, but also in the life and heritage of the working cowboy. For more information on the society, contact:

Will James Society • c/o Will James Art Company
2237 Rosewyn Lane • Billings, Montana 59102

Mountain Press is pleased to make Will James's books available again. Read and enjoy!

JOHN RIMEL

BOOKS BY WILL JAMES

Cowboys North and South, 1924
The Drifting Cowboy, 1925
Smoky, the Cowhorse, 1926
Cow Country, 1927
Sand, 1929
Lone Cowboy, 1930
Sun Up, 1931
Big-Enough, 1931
Uncle Bill, 1932
All in the Day's Riding, 1933
The Three Mustangeers, 1933
Home Ranch, 1935
Young Cowboy, 1935
In the Saddle with Uncle Bill, 1935
Scorpion, 1936
Cowboy in the Making, 1937
Flint Spears, 1938
Look-See with Uncle Bill, 1938
The Will James Cowboy Book, 1938
The Dark Horse, 1939
Horses I Have Known, 1940
My First Horse, 1940
The American Cowboy, 1942
Will James Book of Cowboy Stories, 1951

PREFACE

This is a saga of one cowboy who has rode in the first bucking horse and steer roping contest, the only spectators being cowboys, three herds of over ten thousand to each, six hundred saddle horses, and all the goings on on open range.

This cowboy went from the open range contests on right along to where the contests came to town and was called Rodeos.

This is a story of the Rodeo, and with this one cowboy you will see the inside of the game, from start to today—and if you keep track of Flint as he rides, ropes and bulldogs there won't be no stiff data, but plenty of the action of a contesting cowboy.

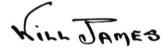

CONTENTS

DRAWINGS BY THE AUTHOR

RODEO PHOTOGRAPHS
AT THE END OF THE BOOK

Cowboys' Bareback Bronk Riding Contest for the
Championship of the World
—Bone

Cowgirls' Bronk Riding Contest for the Championship of the World

It takes good strong hemp fastened to a good horse
to make this steer face you.
—Cal Godshall

Cowboys' Calf Roping Contest for the Championship of the World
—Cal Godshall

Cowboys' Bronk Riding Contest for the Championship of the World
—Cal Godshall

Cowboys' Steer Wrestling Contest for the Championship of the World

Cowboys' Steer Riding Contest for the Championship of the World
—Cal Godshall

Stage coach race

Chuck wagon race

Trick roping

Easy for him—another good roping feat

Trick riding

Single steer roping

A hard landing

Ready for the kill but not for the bull

Find the cowboy

Good pony and good cowboy

This cowboy had no intentions of riding backwards nor so high
—Cal Godshall

Throwed bucking rein and stirrups away

This pony, not satisfied with getting his man down is going after him

No chance for a cowboy here

I

THE FIRST ROUND UP

A COLD NOVEMBER wind was blowing as a cowboy rode down the point of a low ridge to where little of that sharp wind could reach him. There he stopped, got off his horse, shouldered against him like as to keep warmth with him, and with numbed fingers went to rolling a smoke.

His eyes wasn't on his cigarette as he rolled it, they was as had been for many days on a big herd of grazing cattle which he was at the edge of and most always steady watching that none strayed away.

He wasn't the only cowboy doing the same, there was six altogether at different points bordering that herd, and all was well needed, for that herd numbered over ten thousand head. Ten thousand head of mostly longhorn stuff, the rest of mixed, with a showing of the new imported Hereford, all steers, none less than four years old and from there on up to an unguessable age, but all fat as butter after ranging on the grassy northern plains. And they was now ready for shipment.

There'd been a few days of slow trailing to the shipping point, and to allow the cattle to fill and rest up well so as to have all the weight possible on 'em before loading 'em into the cars. For the long steel trail to market one extra day was allowed. The cars had been ordered, five trains of 'em and two engines to each, and now

1

His eyes wasn't on his cigarette as he rolled it.

the big herd was being "loose herded" (scattering) and held ready to within a few miles of the shipping yards, just far enough so the cowboys with the herd could see the water tank by the railroad and hanker to have the shipping over with so they could have their well-deserved fun in the little cow town afterwards. A little of that goes well with any red-blooded human that's seen plenty of hard riding and long hours in the saddle, in all kinds of weather, day and night and from six to nine straight months.

That's a worrying time for the cow boss, to keep all of his cowboys with the herd until the stock is loaded in the cars and shipping is done, for then's when all hands are needed, more so than with the everyday work on the range. It's ticklish work to get the spooky stock in the shipping yards, and one little stampede might mean much loss on the weight of the cattle.

This cowboy at the point of the low ridge and about half froze wasn't worried much about cattle per weight. He was wishing they was all loaded in the cars and on their way, for outside of one day in middle summer, when he bowed his neck and told the wagon boss (cow foreman) that he was going to town wether he liked it or not, he'd been out on the range for eight straight months and sleeping on the ground for six of them months. That was when he could find time to sleep, which was about six hours out of the twenty-four.

So, he was kind of entitled to at least a good plate of ham and eggs for a change, a bath, a change to new clothes, a hair cut on head and face, and then a saunter on for a little fun along with the other boys. Then's when the little old cow town would come to life, and it'd always prepare for it.

But after a few days the fun would wear out, along with his money, and he'd hit for the range again, to some winter cow camp getting snowbound cattle thru drifts and where he'd be good until spring come and round up started again.

After long months of hard riding the cowboy is anxious to have the shipping over with and work done for a spell, but after a long winter of snow bucking he's just as anxious to be on round up again and out of permanent camps.

This cowboy, Flint Spears by name, wasn't thinking of winter camps or roundups as he smoked his cigarette and seen that his part of the herd didn't graze too far out. He was thinking of some ways and means to make his long summer's wages last longer and do better for him than all the times he hit town before. He was thinking on that platter of ham and eggs in a warm restaurant as the first thing he'd get, when glancing away beyond over the earth he seen a long dark ribbon, much darker than the brown earth and about two miles long. It was cattle, another herd, and looked like about the same size as the one he was with. It was just coming in, to ship too.

"Well," thought Flint, "Old Sol Burney and the cow boss of what ever that other herd is should of got together as to their shipping dates,—a bad night, a little stampede and big herds like these so close together would soon mix. It'd sure take plenty of time and work to cut out and get each herd straight again, not counting the poundage that'd be lost in the rounding up and cutting out the expense of keeping the trains waiting. Jumping Jehosphat! That'd sure be some mixup and gathering." He grinned at the thought. "But let 'er go Gallagher."

He watched and then seen that the long herd begin to point away. "That's better," Flint remarked, and by the time it was held it was a good five miles of prairie distance away.

The days being short there was three short "dayherd" shifts, but the night guard shifts made up for that, for the eighteen riders, taking turns of six at a time, stood three hours at each shift, making nine hours of night guard and the remaining hours again split in three shifts for dayherd.

Counting the cow boss, the cook and flunky, horse wrangler and nighthawk, there was twenty-three men with the Seven H. L. 7L herd, an above-average bunch of men of all parts of the cow country, from Mexico to Canada, and Old Sol Burney always prided himself, and boasted when he could, that there wasn't another outfit between the two borders or acrost the both of 'em that had a crew that could begin to compete with his in roping, riding, or handling a herd. He treated his men according and they treated him the same, and even tho his boast had never been called there always comes a time, like with any boast.

Flint had been on the afternoon shift, and when him and the five other riders was relieved by another set of six and rode into camp for supper there was a visitor, the cow boss of the herd that'd just been trailed in and of an outfit two hundred miles the opposite direction of the 7L, it was the "Three T" 𝔗 outfit. They was doing extra heavy shipping that fall, even to fair "she-stuff," and there was around twelve thousand head in their herd, with a crew of twenty-one men.

There was visiting between the two camps that evening, and cowboys who hadn't seen one another, some of 'em for many years, met again and talked over old times.

But as wonders never cease and as good or bad always seem to come in threes, there was a third herd spotted the next afternoon, as big a herd as the 7L or the 𝓨 and "Doggone it," thought Flint, "where was all the stock cars going to come from to handle all this shipping? There'd be a couple of herds due to do some holding, but he hoped it wouldn't be the 7L because this dayherding sure wasn't to his liking."

But Flint didn't have to fret about that third herd because it was a stock herd (cows, weaners, yearlings, etc.) from the Slash A —A outfit and only being shifted to another range further on south to winter.

And that evening while the herds was being held five miles or more apart, representing over thirty thousand cattle altogether, sixty cowboys and four hundred saddle horses was a congregation of bellering, nickering and talking that sure enough went to make it cow country.

All but about twenty men on shift with the herds and "remudas" (saddle-horse bunches) gathered at the 7L camp that evening. A beef had been killed and the three cooks and flunkies pitched in to cooking the supper. A separate big fire was built, for the evening was plenty chilly, and there all gathered around it is where serious visiting talk begin and went on. It got less serious as it went on and more on the joking side. Then a couple of precious mouth organs and mouth harps was dug up and good attempts was made at good old tunes, such as, "That fateful night she wore a rose of white," and the likes.

The older men didn't pitch in with the singing much, they'd listen once in a while but they was more for talking "cow." The most of 'em talked cow all thru the good supper that was spread out in the Dutch ovens, skillets and pots that was by the cooks' fire, and naturally, when you talk cow the cowhorse is brought in, and roping and riding in general.

And naturally, too, that brings on telling of happenings to show how good each man's horse is, or how tough and bad. All depends wether they're cowhorses or outlaws, one is mighty good and the other is mighty bad, either better or worse than the other feller's. There wasn't so much bragging for each man's own roping or riding ability, but one could brag about the other on that, and that was well done.

So well done that as each of the three cow bosses begin bragging about their own riders, is when Old Sol reared up to boast again and made the first offer to bet a hundred dollars that he had the best riders and ropers of the three outfits.

At that statement all the boys quieted sudden. It was a big statement for anybody to make and some call to it was expected. And this time Old Sol didn't get away with his boast, for the 𝍐 cow boss called his bet and raised it to two hundred. Old Sol grinned and grabbed at the chance.

"But we'll do it this way," says the 𝍐 cow boss. "We'll lay a hundred on the bucking horse riding and a hundred on the steer roping, in two separate bets, and that way" he grinned "you *might* make it to win."

Old Sol snorted and agreed. And now something was expected for the ─A cow boss. He didn't seem so very anxious. He thought a while and finally said:

"I'll tell you what I'll do. I'll bet one hundred and fifty, and knowing you won't want to use your beeves for roping I'll furnish the stock for that purpose for the other fifty. I've got some plenty wiry steers, not fat enough to ship but'll sure make fine roping."

That was a decided go and all three shook hands on it. Now, when would the doings be coming off? And that was decided by the cow boss of the stock herd.

"Well," he says, "I've got to move on with my herd and I can't lay over one day. Can't we make it tomorrow?"

They could, and as they went to deliberating about this and that they got to thinking, how about the judges? None of the cow bosses nor any of the cowboys would do because they'd naturally be for their own outfit. It would have to be some neutral judges, judges who wouldn't be favoring any of the outfits.

"I'll tell you what I'll do," Old Sol says sudden. "I have to go to town early in the morning to see about the cars I ordered anyway, and I'll look for somebody there."

"Yes, good idea," says the ⚡ man, "and we'll go with you too because we'll want some say about the picking of them judges."

Old Sol grinned. "All right," he says, at the same time gave the two a nudging look. Then the three walked away from the fire a piece and in low tones begin to confab.

When they got back the cowboys expected some kind of an announcement, and there was. Old Sol looked at all of 'em around the fire, and then he spoke.

"You all heard us doing the betting," he begins, "and now each one of us need the best riders and ropers to back us up. Any of you boys want to come in on this let us know in the morning. Tell the boys that's on shift now the same thing when you boys on the next shift go to relieve 'em.

"Each outfit can only use three for the broncho busting (there was no such term as bronc riding then) and the same for roping steers. There'll be two prizes for each of the doings, fifty dollars for the best and twenty-five for the second best. That's all, boys."

"No, that ain't all," says the ⚡ cow boss, coming to the front. "We don't want any of you boys loping into town tonight when off guard and getting any likker for the doings, not till after the shipping is done, boys, and then you can put 'er on as wild as you want to, and maybe have another riding and roping doings. Now that is all."

Some of the boys grinned under their hat brims at one another at that, but the cow bosses wasn't much afraid of them going to celebrating until the work was done. One or two might go to hankering too strong and being so close to town might weaken, but that happens in all walks of life and with folks that never knew what it is to be away from towns for over a week at a time once a year. The difference is that, during them days, the cowboy might see town for a week only once or twice a year.

Soon as the dayherd shift went on the next morning and the herds was quietly grazing from their "bed grounds"* to different creeks for water the three cow bosses saddled up and headed for the little cow town ten miles away. The first place they headed for when they got there was the freight depot, and then Old Sol found out that his cars wouldn't be there till that afternoon. At any other time he'd of got sort of peeved but this time it was all right, and loading

*Where the cattle is held to bed down during the night.

could be done until the first train was loaded even if it took until away into the night. It's no harder to load at night than in daytime.

That attended to, they rode on the livery stable and told the stable man of what they was looking for and what for. To that the stableman's eye brightened a bit and he says:

"Well I've only rode for about forty years before I got this barn, and I might be some kind of a judge."

He mentioned some of the outfits he rode for and before the long herds begin to be trailed north and that sure qualified him for one judge, but there'd need to be one more and Sol asked the old cowboy stableman where they'd be likely to find that other one.

The stableman didn't hesitate none in thinking of another. "There's the sheriff," he says. "There was a time when he sure used to could stomp 'em, and he could throw a mean loop too. You'll find him either at his office this time of morning or at *Bill's Place*."

Being that *Bill's Place* was the first along the one main street to the sheriff's office, the three stopped there, and there they found the sheriff taking his "morning's morning." His eyes also brightened up some when he was told what was wanted of him. He deputized the bartender right there and then to take charge and he was ready to go.

"There might be a few boys amongst all that bunch that I might want as guests for the State anyhow," he says, "and I'd like to look 'em over."

"If that's the kind of a judge you're going to be," comes back the ⚹ man, "you better stay where you are. You can do your State work after we're thru with these herds."

"Well," grins the sheriff, "I can at least look at 'em, can't I?"

The bartender deputy set up the "poison" for all four, and after some little understanding talk they hit for the stable. The stableman had his own and the sheriff's horse saddled when they got there and all headed for the 7L wagon. Every cowboy not on shift from the three wagons, over forty of 'em, was waiting there when they rode up, and in the rope corral, instead of the regular 7L remuda was the "rough string"* of the three outfits, about forty head of the worst horses in the country to pick from for the bucking horse riding.

The horses that had been kept up and rode in was most all dayherd horses, the few gentle ones in a cowboy's string. They'd be used for "snubbing" the outlaws while being saddled. Then some of the boys that was to rope had saddled the tops of the top horses of each remuda for that purpose. All was well mounted and ready, and now the names of the men that wanted to ride and rope for the prizes had been put on three pieces of paper, one for each outfit, and handed to the cow bosses to peruse.

About all of the cowboys excepting the too old a ones had put their names down on the list, for bucking horse riding or roping, and some for both of the doings. The three bosses had to grin with pride at all the names on their lists.

"Well," the sheriff remarked, as he looked over their shoulders at 'em, "it looks like you're all pretty well full handed."

"Yes," Sol snorts back at him, "and don't you be picking any names off these lists either, not till after shipping anyhow."

*Spoiled outlaw horses.

12

As had been made understood to the cowboys the night before, only six was to be picked out for the two doings (termed event, now days). That was three for bucking horse riding and three for roping from each outfit, and now the three bosses, knowing their men as they did, went to checking on their lists the ones that'd be most apt to do the winning for 'em, their top hands in riding and roping.

There was a few on the list wanted that was on shift and them was sent for and replaced by some whose names wasn't on the list. But a couple of them was wanted for other things, and when they heard that the sheriff was to be one of the judges they sent word back that they'd changed their minds. Others was then put in their places, and when the selection was made and come time for the names to be called there was a hesitation amongst the bosses as to which one was to be the first to do the calling. Then them bosses noticed too that there was worried looks and fidgety actions amongst the cowboys for fearing they'd be left out. That'd be mighty humiliating, for any cowboy that can ride and rope halfways well thinks he's as good as any, his pride is mighty sensitive as to that, and one being chosen and another near as good being left out is a ticklish thing to do, specially with a cow outfit and at shipping time, for the ones left out might get up on their high horses, tell their bosses to go to the hot place and hit for town where there's no telling what they might do if they got on a rampage. As has been in some cases, the police force couldn't compete and neither could the soldiers that was called from the nearest forts, for the boys had to have their fun or their fights whichever way they felt, and it was found out they was best to be left alone, for seldom was there any trouble hunters among 'em.

Thinking all of that over from experience, the three bosses went into another private confab, and when it was over, Old Sol delivered the decision again.

"Well, boys," he begins, "we decided we couldn't pick any six best men out of each outfit. We figured you all to be the best and all rope and ride that wants to. The prizes still stand the same, two for riding and two for roping. Do your best, boys, and may the best men win."

There was no "'Wild West, Whoopees!!'" as that was listened to and taken in, but the show of the sudden vanishing tenseness replaced by broad grins, near like that of a man who's given a chance for his life after being condemned to death, more than made up for any show holler that ever was invented.

The only ones that felt sorry for themselves now was the boys on shift. They'd have to hold their herds to grazing as usual and a good distance away, with not even a chance for a far-away look. But the cooks and flunkies was all on the job at the 7L wagon where the bucking horse riding was going to take place. The nighthawks (night horse herder and wrangler) who should have been catching up on their sleep had no thought for that and was on hand too. Even the day horse wranglers took chances of being bawler out by their bosses, left their remudas on good grass where they figured they'd stay and rode in, hoping not to be noticed, to watch the doings. For that was a day of a lifetime, and no contest, duel, bull fight, game or demonstration could of got any one up on their toes as that range gathering of riders got themselves up in their stirrups. For most all would be riding against one another, and it wasn't only one outfit against the other but rider against rider even with the

14

same outfit, for only the best man won, regardless, and the prize wouldn't be considered with the pride in winning. No gladiator ever entered an arena, and no boxer or wrestler ever crawled thru the ropes with more at stake in their hearts than each one of these cowboys had. It wasn't going to be no knitting doings, only maybe bones afterward.

There was no town folks gathered to see the doings, only the sheriff and the stableman, and they couldn't exactly be called that, for both had sat many a horse for many a year and their "rigs" (saddles) wasn't hung up yet. There was no grandstand only the prairie sod and a horse under each spectator, or the chuck wagon for the cooks and flunkies.

The saddles was most all slick, narrow forked double rigs, loose hackamore on the horse's head, and there was no rules only to sit up and ride. There was no use of mentioning that a rider was scratched out the second he touched the saddle horn or any part of the saddle with either hand. That was the same as being throwed.

Old Sol, being he'd been the leader in saying the first word, gave the word to start in by saying, "All right, boys. I'll call your names as they are on the 7L list. Crockett (the ⭫ boss) and Davis (—A boss) will call their own list for their own riders, and when I call each one of you boys that's with my wagon (outfit) why, doggone you all, *ride, ride* like you know how. You'll be riding for yourselves and the 7L."

At a sign from Old Sol a cowboy rode up, and from the outside of the cable corral dabbed his rope over the head of a smooth-built 7L bay and led him out a-fighting thru a long span of the single cable which was the gate and let down to the ground by a wrangler to let the horse step over and out.

As the bay was led out snorting at the end of the rope, Old Sol called the first name on his list, and another cowboy of his, rope in hand, slid off his horse, picked up the bay's front feet with his ready loop, and the bay stood stock still. He was a wise outlaw, like most all of 'em are in the "rough string." And he knew better than fight the foot rope for he'd run against it many times before, only to a hard fall. That same cowboy then walked up to him and slipped a hackamore over his head, blindfolded him with a gunnysack and handed the hackamore rope to the man who first roped him to now do the snubbing.

He was a wise outlaw like most all of 'em are in the "rough string."

The bay's head snubbed close to the saddle horn, the cowboy took his saddle off the horse he'd been on and, without blanket, slipped it on the bay's quivering back, cinched it well, and watching his eye for a hoof, slid into the saddle without the horse hardly knowing it. The hackamore rope from the snubber's saddle horn was handed the rider while he "felt" of his saddle, and then the blind was pulled off without the bay hardly knowing he'd been saddled and that there was a rider on him.

But that bay cocked one ear and he didn't waste no time blinking at the early-day sun; his head felt free and that's all he needed. He didn't give the rider a chance to get set with a few straight ahead jumps; instead he stuck his nose in the ground from the start, and pivoted there and seeming like begrudging tearing up too much country, stuck in one spot about twice his length, but what little land he took he sure made use of and gave his rider no lead as to wether he was going to fall back, turn over, go thru the earth as he landed or scrape a bird's wing as he went up. He was no spinner, just a good crooked hard-hitting horse that made his rider ride.

The rider rode and he knew he had before he got thru. It was a case of a good rider on a good bucking horse.

II
FIRST FIRST PRIZE

NAME AFTER NAME was called, tough horses was roped, snubbed, saddled and rode or rode at, and all the while there was one cowboy getting nervous, for as the names was called he seen where his had been skipped. His, when he wrote it down was about the fourth on the list, and when the eighth rider came out and still no call for him he figured something was wrong.

Good tough horses came out, good rides was made on the old slick trees, a couple of riders got throwed and the judges was busy marking down one, two, three, erasing, and as another rider would come out they would maybe erase three by one name and put down two or four, all depended how the rider averaged up with the others.*

The ninth horse was roped and made the whale line sing as he was led out. He was a rangy blue roan with a head the size, and about the shape, of a full-grown anvil, looked like about the same weight, too, and when that horse was brought to a fighting standstill for breath is when Old Sol figured the judges needed a breathing spell too. It was during that time that he done a little impressive announcing, to the judges, but also for all present.

"Now, Judges," he begins, "cool your heads a bit, because even tho you've already seen some mighty good riding on some good

---

*Nowadays the marks are a hundred, and deducted from, according to the rider's ability.

ponies,* here's another that'll give you a chance at your ability as to judging good bucking horseflesh and a good rider astraddling it when you see it. Watch close."

Old Sol paused for a minute to let that announcement sink in then he called. "Flint Spears," he says, "this is your horse."

Flint's heart was good or he'd of dropped dead as his name was called following such an announcement, specially after thinking he'd been skipped. As it was it lost a couple of beats as he slid off his horse to claim the rangy blue. Flipping the end of his hackamore rope around his front feet he drawed 'em together and soon had him hobbled, slipped the hackamore and blind on him, and while the snubber held the snorting head close to his saddle horn, Flint eased and had his double rigging on him to stay. He pulled up on his shap belt, drawed his hat down and in another second he'd slipped into the saddle. The snubber handed him the hackamore rein, the blind was jerked off and the fireworks started.

The fireworks was mostly like crooked rockets going up, and earth jarring tons of brick coming down, as the blue turned on his worst. The first few jumps had Flint feeling for his rigging so as to get to sitting and riding. The high, hard hitting, quick and crooked jumps didn't let up, but with all of that, it seemed like by miracle, Flint found his saddle again. He hadn't lost a stirrup during the first eruptions nor had he grabbed leather, so he was safe so far from having his name scratched off the list, and the riding he put on from then on with such a good hard horse to give him a chance to show his ability left that name with a A Number 1 in front of it. The top of the 升 riders.

---

*"Pony" doesn't mean a pony or small horse. It's only an expression, and the horse might easy weigh twelve hundred.

There was a couple more 7L riders done good rides and that ended Sol's list for the bucking horse doings. Crockett of the ⅄ then took his place, begin calling his boys one by one and the riding went on with the ⅄ rough string. He had two more riders than Sol did but even at that they didn't average as good altogether as Sol's men did, all excepting for one who put up as good a ride on as tough a horse as Flint did. He was a little center-fire Oregon buckaroo and there was a A No. 1 put in front of his name also.

Davis of the —A was next, his riders also using the outfit's own rough string, good horses and good riding averaging well with Crockett's but not as good as Sol's and he didn't have a rider to compare with either Flint or the Oregon buckaroo, the only two A No. 1's amongst over thirty who rode, and all the way thru, Sol had the best riders, and one of his men was up and decided on for the second prize. But there was too much of a tie between the two up for the first prize to let it go at that, even tho, all the way thru Sol had won. So, to make a final and satisfactory decision it was decided to have the two winning cowboys ride again. Davis had of course lost out on that bet.

Sol and Crockett picked out the best, or worst horses out of each their own rough string, and the reride went on. Flint's horse was another rangy one, a sidewinding, sunfishing, kicking bucker, about as hard a kind there is to ride if not the hardest. But even tho the hard-twisting jumps wasn't at all regular and sometimes like three pitched into one, Flint's flat quirt played as a rhythm as it popped on the horse's bowed neck near every time he hit the ground. Very few times did the popping miss, and on such a crooked horse that went a long ways to the good of the ride.*

*In rodeos now days the use of the quirt has been stopped, even the fanning with the hat or touching the horse with a hand.

The snubber rode alongside and picked up the pony's
head before he quit bucking and started stampeding.

Flint made a great ride, and when the snubber rode alongside and picked up the pony's head before he quit bucking and started stampeding the A No. 1 mark was still by his name.

The Oregon buckeroo's horse was as tough a one as Flint's was, only a different kind of a bucker again more of a spinner and acted as he'd fall back after each spin, which caused the rider to loosen up on his rigging and put him at a disadvantage for the hard jolts that would follow on. But he rode mighty well, and considering all, even a little better than Flint did, so the judges thought, but considering again, this Oregon buckeroo was riding a center-fire rig which makes it much easier to ride a bucking horse with, it sits more forward on a horse's back and where it misses a lot of hard kinks, where with a double rig it's clamped down to where the rider gets every snapping jolt going and a coming. So taking that under consideration the judges figured that the Oregon buckeroo couldn't done so well on Flint's double rig. Then again, Flint scratched once in a while and used his quirt steady, where the Oregon rider didn't do neither. But all around it was hard to decide, so hard that when the judges gave their decision they left it open for Sol and Crockett to change it. Their decision was A No. 1 for both riders, again a tie.

Old Sol more than reared up at that. "Not by a dam-site!" he bellered. "I will agree that it was pretty close riding but if you won't be partial you will say that Flint done a little the best. Besides, all the way thru," he says to Crockett, "my boys outrode yours even if you had two more than I did."

"But that part don't count," says Crockett. "It was the one best rider of each outfit, not all of 'em put together."

"Well, anyhow," Old Sol went on, "that ought to be considered and I still can't see where the last ride our boys made was a tie. You better admit it, Crockett, when you know doggone well you're beat."

There was a little more discussing on the subject, but finally, again leaving it to the judges, it was agreed that Sol had won, not only all the way thru but even to the last ride.

"But I'll get you on the roping," Crockett comes back at Sol, taking his losing good natured. He more or less had to.

"All right," says Sol, "we'll see, but don't forget you've got Davis to contend with too, and from what I heard of his ropers he'll sure be some contender."

"Yep," agreed Davis. "I think this'll be where I come in."

It had taken a couple of hours to go thru the bucking horse riding, settling on the decision and all, and now the steer roping was next. With that it was decided to give the boys who was on dayherd shift for that morning a chance to see and get in on the doings. Four riders would do with each herd for the time they'd have to hold 'em, and so, four of the boys from the 7L and four from the ⅋ who'd seen the bucking horse doings and wasn't named down for the roping was sent out to relieve the six that was with each herd, and then relieved boys soon come a loping in, all but the two who was sort of shy of the sheriff and the law in general. They was good riders and ropers too.

Counting them, all but ten out of over sixty riders would be in at the doings, the most of 'em taking their turn at roping and the rest at witnessing while helping hold the herd. The cooks and flunkies having no way of getting over to the stock herd and where the rop-ing would of course be held would all ride over in the wood wagon that'd been driven from that outfit that morning and they'd have as good a chance at seeing the doings from that wagon as the cowboys would on their horses.

The horses of the rough strings separated and each string taken back to the remudas of the outfits they belonged to by the wranglers, the cowboys, the bosses, the judges and the cooks all moved on to where Davis' stock herd was being loose herded and to grazing. A "cut" (cut out bunch) of mostly cows and big calves was left out about half a mile from the main herd and to be used as a lead for a steer to hit for when cut out of the main herd to be roped.

Like with the bucking horse riding, there was no set rules as to the roping. A steer would be cut out of the main herd and as the steer got out in the clear and headed for the cut the roper was to give him a fifty yard lead, or pass over the line between the two judges before starting. (The judges was about a hundred yards apart on the line and the line was a deep cattle trail.) One extra throw was allowed each roper if the first one was missed, and it didn't matter how he roped or tied his steer so long as he got his down, the tie was good and would stay. It was all up to that and to the time it took as to who would be the winner, and this judging would be much easier than with the bucking horse doings.

Some of the cowboys went to holding the main herd while a few held the cut, and then two men rode into the herd to begin cutting out a good fast steer as the roper, with loop unlimbered and ready, held his horse still on the outside of the herd, to within a guessed hundred feet of the line and waiting for the steer to cross that line, for he wasn't to start his horse until the steer did cross it. The three bosses and some more of the cowboys sort of formed a wing or fence on both sides from the herd where the steer would be cut out and so he'd be sure to hit for the cut.

All was ready, and this time, being it was his herd, Davis was the first to get his men out for the doings. Taking his stand with the list of them in one hand and his watch and reins in the other he called out the first name, for his cowboy to be ready. Then as that cowboy rode up and took his place and the two cowboys in the herd was given the sign, a lean and lanky "Mexico buckskin" was eased thru the herd and when at the edge, a quick jump from the two riders, a pop of the quirt on shap leg and the wild steer shot out like a bullet. There was no turning back, and when he crossed the cow trail line and the roper jumped his horse after him and the steer seen the cut, he hit for it like a prairie dog hits for his hole, for protection in getting in the middle and mixing with that other herd, the cut.

It took a mighty fast horse to catch up to within roping distance of him, but the roper was riding a fast horse, for at them times there'd already been thoroughbreds shipped in and crossed with mustangs, and the cross made a better and tougher breed than the thoroughbred and they was near as fast. This first roper, like with most of the ropers that would follow, was riding a half breed, and that pony more than et up the distance between him and that fast steer.

But even at that the steer was near over two thirds of the way to the cut before the roper could catch up to within roping distance of him, and then, with his forty foot whaleline, he made a fast and perfect throw over both horns. Now was when a fast horse was needed, to pass the steer as the roper flipped his rope's slack over

25

his rump to go on "yander" and "bust" (throw) him. The horse was fast enough and the busting was well done, for as the horse passed him and the steer went to turn behind, the rope drawed up under his hind quarters, raised him in the air a few feet and flipped him to hit the ground broadside and hard, with his head under him. He hardly no more than landed when the roper was off his horse, by the steer and with his "piggin string" (short tie-down rope) soon had him tied to stay. Then the roper's hat in hand went up for the count of time.

At that the judges and the three bosses was quick to look at their watches to see how many seconds it had taken from the time the steer crossed the line till he was roped and tied and the roper raised his hat and hands. The cowboy had done very good time, considering that there wasn't much practice and such roping to be done with the average day's work on the range, and none of it was done unless necessary. The judges rode over to the tied down steer to inspect the tying and see that it would hold. It was good tying and the roper done the roping and tying from starting line to finish in thirty seconds flat. Davis felt proud and happy and sure that no other cowboy in either of the two other outfits could beat that time.

And that comes out true, for neither of the other two outfits did beat that time. Quite a few come mighty near, to within a few seconds, and made Davis hold his breath. He took a long breath when all the roping was over and his cowboy's time hadn't been beat. But even tho that one cowboy had won first prize and all his cowboys together beat the other two outfits when the time of each cowboy was added up, Davis lost out on the second prize, and the queer part of it was that, again, one of Old Sol's cowboys and one of

Crockett's came to a tie, the same as had happened with the bucking horse riding. Both cowboys had roped and tied down their steers in thirty two seconds flat, not a split second's difference. The three bosses had to laugh at that, and Crockett had to remark to Old Sol:

"Well," he says, "it looks like I have about as good a bunch of cowboys as you have."

"Yes, about," grins Sol, "but not quite."

There'd been a few different throws brought with the roping, like the "Johnnie Blocker," where the loop is sailed to spin in front of the steer and slams back faster than the steer can dodge. That throw can't be made for very far and is used mostly when a steer is crowded and is about to stop sudden and dodge back. Then there was that swift throw where the loop is whirled once or twice and slides off the thumb at the speed of a bullet, a good throw if it can be done and a couple of the boys did. But the regular overhead whirling loop and straight throw was the mostly used.

The "dally" men, the ones who take turns around the saddle horn with their rope instead of tying it, didn't come in on the roping, because dally men seldom "bust" (throw) a critter, they work in pairs when it comes to roping, one "heads" (ropes the head), then the other "heels" (ropes the hind feet) and stretches the critter to lay on the side, for branding or whatever is wanted when an animal is roped.

Being there was so few dally men there was no special doings for them, and being that dallying is a hard trick of its own few dally men will even tackle handling a tied rope, for that has quite a few tricks too and some dangerous ones, even with the cowboy who knows how. So, with the tie-men there'd been some rough goings on during the roping. Some big steers was "busted," raised high off the ground and turned over at the end of the rope before they hit the earth to lay for the tying, a few horns was broke in the falls, and a few necks cracked, but as good luck would have it not a neck or leg was broke during the doings, with near forty head of the wild steers being roped.

But even as lucky as it was, the steers wasn't the only ones that took a little rough and tumble. There was some horses jerked down by the fast and heavy steers, and to land hard on their sides or over backwards. Then there was the cowboys, a few had to do some tall scrambling so's their horses wouldn't fall on 'em, also keep out of the dangerous and entangling coils of their ropes as their horses was jerked down. A couple of the horses got on their feet again with the rope between their legs, and being the rope was tied hard and fast to the saddle horn and a tough wild steer at the other end there was considerable commotion when that happened. A bucking, fighting horse at one end of the rope and the same with the steer at the other end. Any place along that rope wouldn't be no place for a cowboy to be at such a time, for them ropes have a great way of coiling around a feller's neck or body once in a while.

Like did happen with one of the boys. His horse went to bucking soon as he made his catch and the rope tightened. The horse bucked in a circle one way and the steer bellered around another way, no chance for the cowboy to keep the slack of the rope off himself, there was no slack to draw up on, for the rope was kept tight as the whirling and bucking went on and the cowboy rode. And that cowboy had to ride, for the first thing he knew as his horse went to whirling and bucking there was a couple of coils of the rope around his waist and saddle horn, and holding him there, a wild steer's weight at one end tied to a bucking horse at the other end and the cowboy with coils of the rope around his waist in between.

He'd of been near cut in two, or badly hurt, but soon seeing what was going on a couple of cowboys raced up, one caught the horse and pulled his head up, while the other cut the rope.

There was other kinds of happenings, such as many can happen with a rope when there's a wiry steer at one end a horse at the other, a cowboy in the middle and all for him to handle. All was more or less dangerous happenings, for roping is dangerous anyway, even if all goes well, but with that there was some happenings that was also comical, like when one cowboy roped and throwed his steer in good time and went to tie him down. The steer hadn't been throwed hard enough to lay, got up as the cowboy come near and, letting out a beller, went after him. Naturally the cowboy run for his horse, not only to get away from the steer but to get in the saddle and throw him again, but the horse not being any too gentle (or such as the well trained rope horses used in Rodeos nowdays are) turned and started to run too, away from the cowboy and the same way the steer was coming, with the cowboy in the middle, the horse ahead and the steer close behind him.

Well, at that turn of events the cowboy soon seen he had no chance in that race, but for a cowboy he was sure running good, and then, when the steer's long horns was about a foot from him was when he quit the race. He dodged quick and away to one side and fell flat to earth, the steer's head was jerked with the rope at about that time which kept him from turning, and for a ways he had to follow the horse at rope's length. The cowboy was now safe.

The steer hadn't been throwed hard enough to lay.

There was some more goings on before the herd was left to the dayherd men to let scatter and graze again and which wasn't with the doings. One Mexican vaquero (cowboy) took after one long legged steer that quit the herd like for never to return, but as that vaquero got near he run his horse right into him, horse's shoulder against steer's rump, and in such a way that the steer was sort of lifted into the air, twisted and was throwed to turn a couple of good hard summersaults.

When the steer got up on his feet he was kind of dizzy and hardly knew where he was at, and when he finally located the herd he seemed in a hurry to get back to it. But that vaquero wasn't thru yet and before that herd-quitting steer got to it he turned him over once more. When that steer did get to the herd after that he got right into the middle of it. He would never quit it again.

That's a very hard stunt to do and a rider has to break a horse to it before it can be done. But not to be bested, and as another wiry steer broke out, for no reason only that he maybe felt wild, another rider took after him and that steer was also stood on his head and made to turn over a couple of times. With this second rider, who was none other than Flint, he didn't just bump the steer as the Mexican vaquero did, which in itself was plenty hard to do, but he grabbed a hold of the steer's tail, took a couple of turns around the saddle horn with it as the horse bumped and passed him, and that way the herd-quitting steer was well stood on his head and turned over a couple of times, to later on get up again, look around kind of foolish and like wondering what'd happened. That steer was also glad to get back into the herd.

Today's rodeos are not allowed to put on such doings, not even steer roping it for throwing. It's of course not so necessary because there's plenty of action and goings on without that, but on the range, where the cattle are not of the mild eyed breed that comes home to the name of Bossie or the rattling of a bucket, it's often very necessary to herd-break the wildest so they will stay with the herd and can be handled. If left break away as their wild instinct tells 'em, they soon would get so they couldn't be drove or held into a herd, corralled or shipped. They'd get wild, others would follow their lead and in time they'd have to be shot down like game. Then this beef eating nation would suffer considerable.

The doings now all over, the cattle left to scatter and peacefully grazing again, the cooks and flunkies in the wagon hit for camp, the —A camp this time, and proceeded to mix and cook the grub for the noon meal, for it was near that time. On account of there being so many and not enough dishes to go around, there'd have to be a relay on that meal. The 7L and 𝄐 riders and cooks would of went to their own camps, but this was a gathering that very seldom happened and needed a little visiting. Besides, Davis would be moving his herd on right after that meal and make camp again some miles further on before night come.

After a while the three bosses and the two judges come slowly riding to camp while discussing that forenoon's doings. The riders then drifted in by twos and fours, all doing the same, and some just plain visiting or talking of where one or the other would hit for when shipping was done. Whether to stay with the outfit for the winter or to drift on to some other cow-country state where there was no snow to buck was sometimes brought in on the talk, till, as all hit camp and hobbled or picketed their horses, and when all being together that way the talk got more general, then the two judges left the three bosses and went to join the cowboys who now had gathered in bunches and sort of formed a circle around the blazing fire. For this was another cold fall day.

As the sheriff and stableman left, the three bosses went on to discussing about the dividing of the prize money. They'd talked and thought a little about it as they rode in, and now they was on the subject of splitting the prizes between the boys that tied even up in riding and roping.

"Why," says Old Sol, "splitting the prize money that way strikes me like putting the first prize into second and second into third, and to make it fair with our boys I'm not for splitting that prize money on 'em. I'll pay my rider and roper full first and second prize money."

"And I'll do the same doggone thing with mine," says Crockett.

(That's more than could or can be said with any rodeo, and promoters of small rodeos used to once in a while run off with all the money taken in, without paying their contestants the prizes they won, and leaving them stranded.)

"Well," Davis joins in, "I've only got one first prize to pay but I lose a hundred dollars on the bucking horse riding. That makes an even hundred and fifty, boys. Besides, I didn't win the second on the roping, so that makes another twenty-five I lose."

"You don't lose nothing on the betting," Old Sol chirps in; "no more than me and Crockett does. We both have to pay our men fifty dollars each for first prize in riding, even if Flint did win there (grinning), then we both have to pay twenty-five for the second prizes in roping, and me, I have to pay an extra twenty-five, for second prize in riding. This has to be done to keep peace in our families. As for you, Davis, you furnished the steers for roping and after paying the fifty to your man for first prize there you're out about the same as we are. You'd lose a hundred to me and Crockett on the riding, and we'd each lose a hundred to you on the roping if you'd get both first and second, but as it is we owe you about fifty dollars each, just what you owe us on the riding, so it looks to me like the best thing is to call it square and pay our men. We're all three winners and losers, even if my outfit is the best all around."

That last was overlooked, and now, Crockett had something to say.

"Yes," he says, "it looks like we're all square on the betting and that we sure enough don't owe one another nothing, but we're the three of us losers of seventy-five dollars each to our men, and I can't for the life of me get it into my head that we're all losers and each have to pay, pay more than the prizes was decided on at first."

"Why, that's easy enough," says Old Sol. "We agreed to pay our boys their full prizes on account it was an even up tie, and that raises the ante up to near forty dollars for the two of us, Crockett, then none of us won all the way thru. Like if I's won on both doings that would of made six hundred dollars, counting my own two hundred, and figuring it all out, taking off the fifty dollars for the use of Davis's stock, and three hundred in two prizes for both doings that'd leave me be with the whole net amount and winner of fifty dollars."

At that it came to the three mighty sudden that they wouldn't be winning much to speak of if one did win all, and with taking in the two doings, riding and roping, with three outfits competing that'd be as impossible as rowing across the desert in a boat.

"It seems to me like we sure done some poor figuring on this betting and doings," Davis remarked.

"No," says Sol; "we didn't do any poor figuring, we didn't do any figuring. We just all got up in the air about it, and now we just got down to earth."

"Yes, and we each got quite a bump too," says Crockett. "Seventy-five dollars worth."

"And a hundred dollars worth for me," Sol reminded. "One first and second prize in riding, then one second in roping."

The three sat and pondered on the subject for a spell. Finally Crockett spoke up. "There's something mighty wrong about all this," he says.

"There sure is," agreed Old Sol, " and I think I know what it is. For one thing we done the betting between ourselves only, and the other thing is that we went at it without figuring and went to offering prizes to our riders and ropers to carry our bets thru. That's all fine and our doings. But here's what I got to thinking just now, what we should of thought of before, and that is that each one of the boys who want to compete should pay about two or three dollars to get in on each doings. That money wouldn't only go to pay the prizes but it'd sure make every cowboy do his best, like he was betting on himself and to at least get back what money he put in. "What do you think?"

Crockett and Davis thought it over for a spell, Davis thought it was a good idea.

"And I sure think it is, too," says Crockett. "And the next time I pull off any more like this I'll be sure to remember. As it is now it's understood that we're square between ourselves, and all we've got to do is pay our boys."

"Yes," says Sol, sort of dry, "and the judges."

But when the three finally wound up their confab and got a chance to talk to them two, they wouldn't hear of it of being paid for judging, nor for their time or trouble.

"Why, I'd been glad to pay to see what I did," says the stableman.

"Yes," adds on the Sheriff, "and I'd of come out anyhow if I'd heard of it, and now I'm only much obliged to you for letting me know."

So, all figured out and now decided on, the five went on to talk about things in general, the condition of the ranges and stock here and there, the market, and even politics. It had been made understood with the cowboys that the men who was to relieve that forenoon's dayherd men, for all three of the herds, was to eat first, also with the wranglers, the three bosses and the two judges, for the judges would have to get back to town, and two of the bosses to see about the cars they'd ordered. The rest of the men would have plenty of time to eat and visit afterwards.

Soon enough there was a holler from the Davis cook to "come and get 'er," and the ones to eat first begin to make tracks for the chuck box panel for tin plates, cups and utensils. The rounds was made to the Dutch ovens, skillets and coffee pot on coals by the fire, and after another trip to the chuck box for seasoning and such they finally all trailed back to their fire and to squat cross legged around it, full plate between the knees and coffee cup on the ground by the side.

There was little talk during the meal amongst the cowboys, for being they was to relieve the men on dayherd, and it was cow country custom that no time should be wasted, none wanted to be last. The wranglers also had to each get their remuda corralled for a change of horses for all hands before change of shifts, and they wasn't wasting no time mixing talk with eating either. . . . The big fun was over.

III

CONTESTANT SPIRIT

THE SHERIFF and the stableman, Old Sol and Crockett was all riding abreast on the way to town, when about halfways there they met up with the stableman's helper. He'd got word from the shipping agent that part of the stock cars, about half of what Old Sol had ordered, was on the way and would be at the shipping pens that afternoon, the rest of 'em would be along early the next morning. There was no word as to Crockett's order, but it was expected there might be most any time. Freight, wether it was stock or cotton, didn't move very fast then.

Only one herd could be shipped at a time anyhow, and as Old Sol and Crockett left the sheriff and the stableman and rode back, the two come to an agreement where Crockett would furnish all of his men but them on shift and help Sol load his herd. Sol would do the same for Crockett when his cars come, was loaded and gone.

That was a great help to both outfits, and that afternoon five thousand of 7L steers was brought in to the shipping pens and a couple of thousand of 'em inside and ready to load. That's all the pens could hold, and it was ticklish work corralling the spooky, fat cattle but there was around thirty good cowboys on the job, and as good luck would have it the wide gate had just been closed on the first bunch when the smoke of the coming train was seen. They'd been harder to corral if the train had already been there.

It was ticklish work corralling the spooky, fat cattle.

It was good too that there was three loading chutes at the big yards, for sometimes the cars was the right length so all three of the chutes could be used, and most of the time two of 'em. So, with all the help, only five of the men to hold the cattle that couldn't be corralled, the loading went pretty fast.

What population there was of the town was near all out to see the cattle and the loading of 'em; they come afoot, on horseback, in buggies and wagons, and barking dogs came along too, which all sure didn't help with the holding, corralling and loading of the cattle. But sundown come and then dark, and most all disappeared.

The first long train was loaded and it pulled out, and before the next train pulled in another bunch of cattle about the same size of the first was corralled and the loading went on. The little town along the track a ways was about dark and most all asleep by the time that second bunch was loaded into the cars. But soon as the second long train-load pulled out and the rest of the cattle that'd been brought were penned in so there'd be no more to hold, Old Sol decided, and Crockett and all the boys more than agreed with him when he mentioned coffee and vittles.

"But there won't be no raising Cain or drinking, boys," he says. "We've got along without that for six months or more, and we ought to be able to stand it for another day or two. Let's throw a quick bait at a restaurant, get out and load up this last bunch. Then we'll hit for camp and the soogans."

That being fine and hunkydory with every one, they all loped into town and tied their horses up wherever they could by or near the restaurant. But there was more tie racks in front of saloons than there was in front of restaurants and the two cow bosses was some worried when they seen a few of the boys hit for one of the saloons. But soon enough all but a couple of 'em showed up, and that was good.

The boys was surprised when as all walked into the one Chinese restaurant they seen that they'd been expected, and all was set and ready. A platter of ham and eggs and a pot of steaming coffee was on the tables each set for six, and all went to make away with that. The coffee pots suffered the most, but there was always more ready, and it was found out before that warming meal was over that Old Sol had sent a rider in to order all this a half an hour before.

There wouldn't be no celebrating now, not after being treated the way they had and not until after the work was done, and before all left a few of the boys went to get the two that'd gone astray, got 'em out and back to the yards before they was too far gone.

With the train waiting and ready, it didn't take so long to load it, but it was time for the "graveyard shift" (midnight) by the time the third long train was loaded and it pulled out.

And the work still wasn't all done for some of the boys. All night horses had been caught up and picketed and there was six riders on each outfit that was up to stand two hours night guard yet, before they could hit the soogans, only with the 7L. Four men would do now, as that herd had been cut to half with the shipping. But to even things up Sol was now short six men, for he'd sent two men with each train-load to unload and reload at each feeding point on the way to market, also to inspect each car whenever the train stopped for any length of time and to prod up any of the cattle that might be down, wedged so they couldn't get up again and would be trampled. Sometimes the cowboy would have to get inside of the car to get one up, and while hanging on to the side would walk on wild backs and amongst wild horn shaking heads to get to the one that was down. There'd be mad bellers and tail swishing as the cowboy's high and small-bottomed boot heels would go from one back to another, and it wouldn't be healthy for him if he happened to lose his hold on the side of the car, slip and fall in amongst 'em.

When the critter that's down is reached is when the prod pole is used to make room so it can get up. Usually not much room can be made, for cattle are packed tight in the cars so they're less apt to get down. They're loaded that way for other reasons, too, like for warmth while crossing the long, cold stretches of bleak plains, also to of course cut down on the shipping bill, and it ain't so very often that a cowboy has to get inside the cars to get a critter up, with handling his prod pole thru the slats he can most always do that from the outside.

The freight trains moving so slow during them times, there was three places from the 7L range to market where the trains stopped and the cattle was unloaded into big feed yards where the ganted cattle would fill up on hay and water, and be given a chance to lay down for a spell. In a few hours they'd be loaded again, with help furnished by the feed yard companies. Them helpers, with prod in hand and at the loading chutes was called "cowpunchers." There's where that name started, or originated, in the shipping and feed yards and with the first shipments of the longhorns from the Western ranges to the eastern markets. Many of them first cowpunchers, mostly young fellers, turned out to be good on the range afterwards, but the name stuck, and today, cowpuncher stands for the same as cowboy or buckeroo.

When shipping time comes the well-set and regulated routine that goes with the work on round up and most range work is pretty well all upset. A cowboy might not be in the saddle for a straight twelve hours, and then again, he might change horses three times and it might be eighteen or twenty-four hours straight before he gets a chance to let his saddle rest.

Like it was with the boys who'd went on dayherd shift that noon. It was now past midnight, their dayherd shift had run into the "cocktail" hours (from five to eight o'clock herding and grazing to bedground for the night, but no cocktail) then run into nightguard shift. They'd had no supper and no change of horses, and now even the cooks had to be up once in a while and keep the grub warm for whenever they'd ride in. That don't go well with any roundup cook, for he usually has to get up in the small hours of three in the morning.

But the cowboy, *the kind that is*, and deserves to be classed with the real meaning and all that name takes in, doesn't let such goings on bother him any. He don't even think about it and takes the weather, rain or snow, night or day along the same with his work. A fresh horse once in a while is the main thing and goes near as good as a meal when there's hard riding to be done, for a fresh horse will rest a tired rider, and a cowboy can go a long time without eating or resting then and not mind. There's no hard riding on dayherd, only maybe to trot out once in a while and turn a bunch that might be grazing too far. They'd been watered at the creek where the cattle was that evening, and so, the boys that had been on shift since that noon still had about the same as fresh horses when they was relieved on guard that night.

It was still dark when breakfast was et as morning come, barely daybreak when the night horses was turned in the remuda that'd just been corralled and fresh horses was caught. Then the rest of the 7L herd was slowly put on the move, and by sunup was only a couple of miles from the shipping pens. Crockett and his cowboys caught up about then, and soon enough the pens was again filled with another two thousand head of good big steers, just as the smoke of a train was seen in the distance. Empty cars had been brought in during the night and the loading went right on.

The last of the 7L beef steers was loaded a little after noon that day, three more train-loads of 'em, and two more men riding the caboose of each train and going along. Flint was one of 'em, on the last train to pull out. And now there come word that Crockett's cars would be in late that night and he could start loading early the next morning.

Until that time the remaining 7L cowboys, even tho not tired, could rest. So could the ✝ boys, excepting when on shift, but there was plenty of men, the shifts was far apart and there was nothing to do in the meantime but eat and sleep, or maybe go to town. But that last was out of the question, until all cattle was loaded and on the way, and then it was up to each one to do as he pleased. Each one could now, for that matter, but it was against cowboy principle at such a time, when most needed, and few would ever break loose.

It took all the next day and away into the night to get the herd loaded and on its way, and as the red lights on the caboose of the last train disappeared and not a beller could be heard the cowboys felt sort of lost, like as if everything had been taken away from 'em in realizing that they was thru, their work was done. And now that they felt free to go to town none seemed to be in a hurry. When they did ride in they rode slow, and this time tied their horses in front of a saloon, but close to the restaurant. A couple of drinks went the rounds with most of 'em, some three, and a few none, and then one or a few at a time, till most all was accounted for, wound up at the restaurant for some more ham and eggs and coffee, which all, excepting the coffee, a cowboy never gets on the range.

Many of the town's citizens stayed up and gathered around that night and a few tinhorns had floated in along with other kinds of their breed, but there wasn't much drinking with the boys after the meal. There wasn't enough doing in that town anyway, too small, and another big set back was they hadn't got their time checks as yet—

So the most of 'em rode back to camp early enough that night, and the rest came in by twos and threes early in the morning, and as they rode, now well realizing their work was done, no guard to stand that night nor until away in the next spring, they was glad. The cold wind they faced made 'em more so, the sky was heavy and cloudy and there was a feeling of snow in the air. When they woke up the next morning a good blanket of it covered their bed tarps and the prairie sod. It was time to pull in for the winter, or pull out, south.

Most of the cowboys, having their own horses, rode back to the headquarters ranch, to get them in from the range where they'd been free to run all summer, also to get their pay check, if they didn't want to stay on, or there was no work for them. Others got their checks from their cow boss at the wagon and rode back into town, with their beds squaw-hitched on an extra company horse (the horses would be brought back by another rider that day). Some of the boys would be galivanting around for a few days in a bigger town, get some winter clothes and maybe return to the outfit later for a winter job at its many cow camps. It's always hard to tell where the ones that drifted on would wind up at, but it was a pretty safe bet that sooner or later, near or far, they'd be on some other range and riding some more.

With Flint now going with the cattle and riding in the caboose, sleeping and eating there with the other cowboy and brakemen, jumping out night and day to look into each car whenever the train stopped long enough, him along on one side of the train while the other cowboy went along the other side, seeing to the feed and water, unloading and loading at each feed yard and all he didn't get much chance to rest, celebrate or figure out what he was going to do until the train got to the other end and the cattle was delivered in the right hands. That well taken care of he was thru with his responsibility and felt free to do as he wished. He had a return pass, and his expenses in connection with the handling of the cattle and return would be paid by the 7L. But there was no hurry, that stood good for a good length of time, much longer than he'd care to stay in the big livestock market City, but him and the other 7L cowboys that was there would take on the sights for a while, and he would figure out afterwards what would be next.

It would of course be *back to the range* again, and as Old Sol made it understood and said when he left with the cattle:

"Have your fling in the big town, Flint. You've worked hard since the wagon pulled out away last spring, you've been a good hand, and you deserve some sightseeing and fun for a spell. Come back here when you get thru and I'll put you on the main camp at Willow Creek. There'll be a couple of riders there with you, two hay shovelers and a cook."

The Willow Creek cow camp was a long three-room log house with kitchen in center and would be a fine place to ride from and come back to after every day's circle in looking for and bringing in any cattle that would need feeding, and Flint would like it there. But that cowboy was no home guard, and even tho he was only a little over twenty it'd been five years or more since he'd left his home grounds. He didn't leave on account of any trouble or that he didn't like it there. It was just that he wanted to see what it looked like on the other side of the far away blue ridges around him.

He'd covered many ranges and rode for many horse and cow outfits, and kept a drifting on. It wasn't just plain shiftless drifting or grub line riding with him, and even tho he was particular as to what kind of an outfit he rode for his horses seldom got leg weary before he again went to riding for some outfit to his liking, and as he drifted on from outfit to outfit that way his experiences with each, in different range countries and ways of handling stock, was of more value to him as a cowboy and later on a cowman (stock owner) than staying with one outfit or so and work for a raise in wages and maybe a cow foreman's job.

Flint was well liked on the 7L range and that liking went the same with him. He liked the country too, well timbered and watered range land, with rolling hills and grassy plains. And now he was recognized as the best rider of that country. The 7L was mighty proud of him, and he could of rode on in the glory of that fact. But the hankering that always hit him every fall and spring, and sometimes oftener, to drift to new ranges left him sort of undecided and, well, he'd figure it out later, but he'd already decided, without his realizing, that he wouldn't be bucking snow or breaking trail for no stock that winter.

So that's how come that when he got tired of the big town and winter did hit the 7L range, he was quite a few hundred miles to the south of it and riding where only a little sprinkles of rain would come during winters. But it snowed deep in the high mountains by the long and wide valleys, and the hard packed snows, like reservoirs, kept the scattered springs in the valleys running during the dry summer months.

Flint liked that country and soon got a job there, on one of the oldest horse outfits and to breaking horses. That's what he wanted and there was no end to that job, if he could do it well. He done it well and come acrost many good tough horses as he roped and rode one after another every day. He didn't have to be particular about breaking these horses, just took some of the rough and buck out of 'em, the shipping to where they was sold tamed 'em some more, and there was where they was "finished" (thoroughly broke) for whatever use was wanted of 'em. Most of these was half thoroughbred horses, but being crossed with the mustang and raised on the range made 'em as wild as the mustangs themselves, and harder fighters.

With the first of the breaking as Flint was doing the horses was handled and rode on an average of one hour a day, and each horse that way, from eight to twelve saddlings before he would pass as fit to ship, it depended on the horse. And Flint was at the height of his glory with such a job, for he didn't like to finish a horse that took too long and too much learning before they would be called finished, or well broke. The changes of horses didn't come often enough and the breaking would have to go on with working the horse in handling herds.

That would of course be for cow horses but these he was breaking for this big horse outfit, the Cross S (ꝋ), was for use on bridle paths or roads of thickly settled eastern states. They didn't have to be broke to neck-rein or any such like, and so long as they stood while getting on 'em, went well afterwards and stopped when wanted to that's all that was necessary. They was called riding horses then.

The horses that wouldn't break well enough to sell after ten or twelve rides was kept with the outfit and for the cowboys to ride and do their work on. Then they'd sometimes be shipped later on, if they were gentle enough. Some of 'em would never gentle, and for that reason only good riders could hold a job on the ꝋ.

Flint near lived in the big juniper corrals that winter. Another rider was breaking horses in the same corrals with him and the two was in a steady good natured contest as to which one could outdo the other, sometimes winding up by one or the other getting throwed, thru pure recklessness. It was about nip and tuck as to their riding ability, but even tho the other rider was a little older and had more experience, Flint was still a shade the better. He knew it too, could see it in that rider's eyes, and that pleased him a considerable, for, for no reason that he could guess, only maybe his pride, he wanted to be the best rider wherever he rode. He was about that now, and plenty good enough to satisfy most any rider, but, as he thought to himself, some day he would be a *good* rider, and what that meant was beyond any idea of what any man might think good riding was.

But when spring came, after taking the rough off near two hundred head of horses, the most of 'em doing a fair job of fighting and bucking, and some doing a considerable more than just good, he got to thinking he was doing better and more to his idea of what he called riding.

When he left the ⅄ early that summer, for no reason again that he could think of only to be crossing some more ridges to other ranges, he felt more confident as to his riding ability and that he wouldn't have to take his hat off to many, if any. It wasn't that there was any inferior feeling with Flint. It was that he'd seen some powerful good riding now and again ever since he could see, and more later when he left the home grounds and lined out to ride on strange ranges. That had stuck to his mind when mighty young and his aim had been to be as good as he figured as they was. He didn't think there was any more such good riders and the reason for that

Sometimes winding up by one or the other
getting throwed, thru pure recklessness.

he hadn't struck any who could outride him the last couple of years, and he didn't realize that he himself was now as good as the riders whose riding he'd admired and wanted to do as well.

Being the best rider amongst over sixty of a top average of range riders while with the 7L and when the three outfits gathered, pleased and made him feel proud, but he'd put off wanting to believe what a rider he really was by thinking he hadn't rode against such good riders or he wouldn't of won, when, in fact, they was mighty hard to beat. That little Oregon buckeroo who'd rode to such a close tie to him had put up the same kind and as good a ride as he'd watched and admired before, but when he outrode him he couldn't see so much to it and he didn't think it was so much of a feather in his hat to barely beat him.

Flint kept a stingeing himself from any credit that way and kept a finding flaws with his riding while others only had tall talks and looks of admiration for it. At times he'd get to thinking he was in a rut and not getting any better when, in truth, it'd only got so no horse bothered him. The hardest had come easy for him and no new twist or jolt in a buck surprised him. It'd only draw a pleased split second of interest, while that same jolt would of throwed many a good rider. Fact was that Flint got so used to whatever might happen under his saddle it was just as simple and easy as rolling a smoke, with no more thought to it than that.

In many cases it's said that the artist is born and can't be made, when sometimes in them cases the artist, even to the painter or singer, is really trained and made. Bucking horse riding, to do it well, is an art, and one art no man can be trained to or made to accomplish unless it's in him. It's a true born art, like it has to be with the painter or singer in order to be good at it. And at riding is where Flint was a sure enough artist.

There's an art to most every game, but bucking horse riding is one rough art that can't be beat or got around. A cowboy can be raised in the saddle, spend a life time riding and still never be able to ride an ordinary bucking horse. Such cowboys make up for that by usually being good ropers and knowing so much there's to know about cattle and range, which makes them as valuable and as much of a cowboy as the good rider. And the other way around, it's not often that a good rider is much of a roper, the average does well if he catches a horse or whatever he ropes with the second throw.

Like with Flint, being a top rider, he missed his first throw on the steer while at the cowboy doings with the 7L. He caught him with a second throw but his time, after tying, was near one minute which put him well out, for the winners made it in thirty and thirty two seconds.

But Flint wasn't worried so much about his roping and even tho he done a lot of it and tried hard he seen there was no use. He couldn't be no better no matter how much he tried. His aim was for riding, there's where his talent layed and there's where he shined.

With his leaving the 𝓱 it wasn't only to see what was on the other side of the distant blue ridges, it'd got so the good natured contest that had been between him and the other rider had come to an end, Flint had got so good by the time spring come that the other rider couldn't keep up with him, and so, there could be no more contesting. That rider came right out with it and, with a grin, told him so, and at that Flint once again figured that that cowboy couldn't be such a good rider or he couldn't of outrode him.

With that at the back of Flint's mind, and even tho not strong enough for him to realize it, was the main reason for him leaving the ᚥ, to see if over the distant blue ridges he could ride in amongst what *he* called "good riders." He came up onto and rode for a couple of outfits where there was good riders but he soon rode on, for being they couldn't hold a candle to his riding he once more figured they wasn't such good riders either.

There was no stuck up airs or superior feeling with Flint on account he was top rider wherever he rode, for he still thought there was better riders than him, and he was only sort of surprised and disappointed that he couldn't come acrost any so, as he'd say to himself, get a few pointers and learn how to really ride.

That fall he finally struck one outfit where he figured was some sure enough riders, that at least two of 'em was well worth watching, and there, with that way of his, not professing to be a top rider while being one, made him being looked up to the same as he did with the other riders, and he was happy. A good string of rough ponies was handed him, and when the cow foreman seen that as he changed from one horse to another during the day's riding how the spoiled ones was only play to him, he came to him one afternoon when the work was done earlier than usual, there was time to while away, and Flint was where the spring water run by below camp, washing a few clothes.

He squatted across the little stream from him, rolled a smoke, passed a couple of remarks, and then he begin on the subject he really came to see him about.

"I've been watching you," he says, "and it looks like that string I handed you is sort of easy, too easy for you, and I got to thinking you might get stale on such kind. We'll be on the horse range again in a couple of days, and if you want I'll pick you out a string I think will be more to your style. They're good horses but on account of their slippery ways, few could ride 'em and little work could be got out of 'em I've had to cull 'em out from year to year and now they're packing nothing but solid fat and steady accumulating on orneriness. I'd sure like to have 'em rode, then I could be proud to say that I'm the only foreman on the Forty-five (45) outfit who has good enough riders so that all, to the worst of the horses are being rode. It's never been done before that I or anybody knows. These horses have the reputation of being the worst in the state, and they are."

"I take it," says Flint, looking up while wringing a sock, "that none of the boys want 'em and you want me to take 'em."

The foreman grinned a little. "You guessed right," he says. "The boys don't seem anxious for 'em, but I don't know as I blame 'em because these are not just plain bad horses. Besides I don't think they can handle 'em, and I was sort of waiting and hoping a rider would come along that could. From watching you every day I know you can.

"But," the foreman went on, "before I ask you and before you think it over and decide wether you want to take 'em on or not I want to tell you the story of these horses and how we've got the toughest worst horses in the U.S.A., and that of course covers all the horse world.

"It was all due to one stud horse (stallion) they're the breed of. That stud came with a bunch of old Mexico horses this outfit bought some years ago. Nobody knew or could guess what breed he was, but he was a well built and good sized horse so he was kept as a stud and turned out with a nice bunch of mares.

"Whatever that horse was, he sure had the strong blood in him; every one of his colts looked and was marked like him, had the same good action and all of his orneriness. But he was considerable more than ornery and he sure lived up to his name. His name was "Morte" and being he was so fast he was mighty dangerous to any horse and rider that came near his bunch, and that's how come one day he run into a full load of buckshot.

"Some plow pusher from away down the valley country had lost a mare which drifted out here on our horse range, and right away, Morte hazed her into his bunch. When this valley feller finally found her in that bunch some time later and tried to cut her out, the ignoramus, not noticing the dangerous look and shake of Morte's head, started to ride into the bunch to try to cut out his mare as tho the bunch was so many milk cows of his, and then's when Morte interfered.

"When the dust settled and Morte hazed his bunch away this feller's poor little old stove-up and half-starved horse layed dead. We figured he was better off. As for the gallussed sod buster he terrapined his way to one of our camps, he was pretty scared and well battered up, and as he was being bandaged up some he told the boys of the happening.

"The boss there then told him he should of knowed better than trying to cut out any one mare out of any stud bunch, especially Morte's stud bunch. He told him too that they'd be gathering horses soon and he would get his mare then and hold her for him.

"But it was more than a month before the horses was gathered, and when one day during the roundup a rider brought a stud bunch with some of Mortes mares in it it was figured something sure was wrong, because that horse was the boss on that range and could hold his bunch against any other stud. He was found dead a couple of days later, full of buckshot, and it wasn't hard to guess who'd killed him. Besides, that hawnyawk's mare was missing.

"Nothing was done about it because Morte's usefulness was over with on that range anyway, and it'd been decided to trade or sell him. Then again, that weed raiser had suffered some losses and considerable battlement, so the whole thing was overlooked. But we did hope that his mare would have a colt by Morte and that he'd take as much after him as all his other colts did. He'd even things up for his dad.

"Now this special rough bunch of horses I'd like to have you take on are all Morte's colts, they range from eight to twelve years old now and every one of 'em is good for at least twenty years. Them other colts of his that broke, well, about half of 'em, are the best all around cowhorses there is on this range or in this country or, I'll bet, anywheres."

At the word "bet," Flint had to grin to himself. It reminded him of the bet between Old Sol, Crockett and Davis to the north, and he thought at that that a bet on which outfit had the best all around cowhorse would of been good doings along with the other things at that time.

"And," the cow foreman went on, "them ones what didn't break well and got too tough would turn out to be as good a horses as the others that did once they can be rode well and handled right. They might hurt a man but no man can hurt them, not with work.

"So now that I've told you about these horses and given you fair warning you can think it over before deciding as to wether you want 'em or not and let me know before you get to see 'em. I'll only tell you that they're fine horses, as bad as they are. They're no scrubs, and you sure won't be afoot if you can ride 'em."

Flint didn't hesitate or think it over. "I'll take your word for them horses," he says, "and if they're as good as you say they are I'll be glad to take 'em on."

The cow foreman's eyes matched his grin as he stood up, stuck his hand out acrost the little stream and shook on it with the cowboy.

"They're yours," he says, happy, "and there's twenty-five dollars a month more in it for you—But boy," he grinned, "you'll sure have to do some powerful tall riding."

"That's what I hire out for," Flint grins back at him.

IV
THE COWBOY CONTEST
FIRST COMES TO TOWN

WHEN A COUPLE of days later the outfit got near the horse range for a change to a fresh remuda, and Flint got to see the Morte horses, all straight dark bays with a snip on their noses and one or two white hind feet, he was mighty pleased with the general looks of 'em, only thing was they all looked so much alike that it was hard to tell one from the other.

"Guess we'll have to put a different earmark on each one of 'em so we can tell 'em apart," grins Flint.

Twelve head of the fat snaky bays was cut out and put into another corral with part of the fresh remuda that had already been put in there, and as the boys seen the tough Morte horses being run in along with the others to be used some of 'em got a little nervous, and it was a great relief when later on they heard the foreman speak to Flint and asking him if twelve of them horses would do him for a starter.

That relieved feeling turned to interest and wonder, wondering how this new hand, Flint, would get along with that goshamighty rough string. It'd sure be fun watching.

But if it was fun for them to watch as the range work went on, it was as much fun for Flint to ride and put them wiry horses to work.

There was times of course when some of them horses called on for all his talent and natural ability as a rider, but that he welcomed and he once remarked after stepping off one of the worst in his string that a feller sure can't learn to ride on a hobby horse.

"Yeah," says one of the old cowboys within hearing, "but give me the hobby horse in preference to them. I wouldn't want to better my riding that bad."

All was peaceful with Flint that way, and even tho there was some jealousy amongst a few of the best riders, he wasn't worried, for he seen once again that he was sure outriding 'em, and the only thing that kept him from moving on as he realized that fact was the good rough practice them Morte horses was giving him, too rough for many a good rider.

Out of the twelve outlaws in his string there was only two he couldn't get any work out of. Them two had to be throwed for every saddling and fought and bucked so much that they'd tire themselves all out and afterwards would only sulk. They couldn't be rode out to any circle (ride) or any work done with 'em. With the others it was more of a case to be able to set on 'em, and Flint done that and gradually got 'em to behaving some, also in a month or so got the other two lined out to work, a little.

In a couple of months' time, Flint had the tough horses lined out enough so, as the foreman thought, they'd do to divide up with the other riders. That was done, and Flint was sent back to the horse range with another rider and to get twelve more of the Morte spoiled geldings. But it didn't work well with the dividing of the first twelve with the boys, for them ponies went right back to acting the way they had before Flint got 'em. The boys was throwed high wide

Them two had to be throwed and tied down for every saddling.

and skelter and that held up the work a considerable in running 'em back into the remuda and catching 'em again. Consequences was that they all but a few was handed right back to Flint again, and, if possible, more spoiled than ever before. So Flint took most of his second string back to the horse range and went on riding the ones that'd been returned to him, along with a few he'd kept from the second string, and to make up the twelve.

As that went on and riders dropped by the **45** camp every once in a while was when Flint's fame as a wizard of a rider and riding to a standstill any of the often heard of Morte outlaws begin to spread for hundreds of miles around. Flint worked on with them ponies on thru most of the winter and he didn't get much headway with 'em. He'd have some where he figured they'd do well for any good cowboy to go on working with, but a week or so later after the cow foreman would distribute 'em amongst his riders there'd be a return of the old wickedness come back and then eight out of ten of them wild eyed ponies was turned back to Flint again, for another spell of him taking more rough off of 'em.

With all his pleasure in handling such horses, the kind that made him ride considerable more than the average he'd run acrost before it took him longer to get the hankering to move on with his back-of-the-mind hunt to come up against a rider who could outride him, and so he could learn how to really ride from watching him. For the **45** riders wasn't drawing any look from him no more.

Spring comes early in that close to Mexico border country. Far as that goes there was little or no winter, not enough to dampen Flint's eyebrows, and as the hankering to drift again begin to get strong with him then is when rumors and news which stirred up a sudden interest in him made him hold on for a spell. It was that there was to be a cattlemen's convention or gathering where they'd unite and discuss most everything regarding cattle, range holding, standing against rustlers and all such like. These cattlemen would drift in from many states and gather at one of the biggest border towns.

Big news of that came from one with the entertainment committee that was to show the cattlemen what this particular state had to offer in the line of a little interesting doings while resting between meetings, after hitting the bar a little. And being the 45 Morte string had such a reputation as the toughest and at last one cowboy had been found that could set 'em, there was another outfit showed up that claimed the same, with horses and riders, and would put 'em up against the 45's horses and riders. The entertainment committee man grinned and remarked that the other outfit was due for a fall but there was a fair sized bet put up by 'em and it would be easy pickings for the 45, thought the committee man, besides making mighty good entertainment for the visiting cattlemen.

That, when Flint heard of it, of course took all notion of his drifting, for a spell at least. The foreman was pleased as a couple of men in a democrat drove up to the round up camp, one evening and layed down their cards as to the challenge from this other outfit. They was committee men, and realizing that a busy cow outfit on round up can't very well drop work and go galivanting around to do any entertaining a fair sum was offered for the 45 outfit to furnish some of their worst horses and a few of their best cowboys to accept the challenge from this other outfit and all have it out in town for the benefit of the visiting cowmen, who all as the committee men said was big outfit owners or superintendents gathered there from many states around.

"It would be a great honor for either the 45 or the other outfit to win in this contest and would spread pretty well thruout the cow country from the south to the north," says one of the men, "and I don't think the 45 outfit would have any trouble winning."

The 45 foreman would of accepted the challenge without pay but he figured that that money could be well used to bet with. The prize moneys for the winning riders would be paid by the committee, and that went well.

The 45 superintendent, being he was also to be at the convention and connected with the doings amongst the four hundred or more cowmen to be gathered, was all for the doings and accepting the challenge. And so, that's how come that some days later the worst of the Morte bunch of outlaws was picked out, near twenty of 'em, and started for the border town a hundred miles away. Driving them was six of the 45's best riders, and of course, Flint was one of 'em. The foreman left the straw boss in charge of the rest of the outfit to keep the work going some and he went along too.

A few gentle horses packed with beds and grub was taken along and after three days the outfit reached the town and made camp near the stock yards, where the horses was held and fed.

The other outfit's horses and riders came in the next day. The picked worst horses and best riders of the Fiddle (𝄢) outfit, and they looked for all they was.

Flint and the other 45 riders sized it up well, and figured there'd sure be good competition and both sides would sure have to ride for their money, but if anybody was worried, Flint wasn't. He was just plain interested, and as the two outfits pitched fire together that night and all got acquainted there was a grinning but tense feeling, and after all crawled under their tarps there was some of the boys rode all kinds of twisting buckers thru the night.

On account of such special doings as the bucking horse contest, and being the two outfits had put themselves out to be there the convention meetings was held off on the afternoon of the next day. The *Enterprise* had announced as to when and where the doings would be held, and so, at that time and place, all of the visiting stockmen and the town's people was on the job a long time ahead for a good spot to watch the goings on from.

Being there was no arena nor grandstand for the doings it was decided to be pulled off in the main street (no pavements then) and in front of the Los Visitadores Hotel. The windows from there and other buildings close would do well for the ladies to watch from. As for the visiting cowmen, most all the wagons, democrats, buggies and buckboards that could be gathered made up for their box seats and formed a good circle, as a good sized arena. The rest of the town's folks wedged in wherever they could, between rigs, on roofs, trees and wherever they could get a look-see. There was a mighty big crowd, like sprouted from everywhere and on up. It seemed so to the cowboys, and the sight of so many staring faces made 'em a heap more nervous than any thought of the tussle they'd have to put up with their bucking horse riding.

But as the first two or three outlaw horses was led in, snubbed and rode and the contest really started, the crowd was pretty well forgotten and it got to seeming like just so many posts or corral bars.

The three picked judges got to be the only ones any attention was paid to.

As it had been with Flint's first contest while with the 7L there was no set rules as to the bucking horse riding, only to ride as a good rider should ride, without "touching leather" (grabbing) quirt and scratch* and ride straight up.

And as it had been with Flint's first contest he was again the last of the 45 riders to be called. So far, the 45 outfit was well ahead as to the best riders and worst horses. There was no beating that Morte string of outlaws for orneriness and action, and that was well recognized. Now it was up to Flint to wind up the job of winning straight thru against the 8 outfit by outriding that outfit's best rider, who'd also been kept to the last.

For size and general appearance it would of been hard to tell at little distance as to which was which between that rider and Flint. Both was of medium height, wiry slim, dark and had the same action. There was a good resemblance too, only at a closer look there was scars on this other rider's face which ended the resemblance right there, and he was some older.

He was the first one of the two to be called to ride, and as that cowboy slipped into the saddle, Flint knew at a glance that here would be a ride that would call for all of his watching.

Which it did, and then some. For with all the good riding Flint had seen and done himself he was sure enough surprised, and surprised at himself that he was surprised. This riding he was now witnessing was of the kind that'd keep him drifting from one outfit to another in looking for, and now there was again the same look of

*An expression of action and of no harm to the horse.

admiration as there'd been in his eyes while he was a kid and watching some good riding, hoping that some day he could do as well.

Before the ride was half over he seen that now he'd sure have to get to really riding to even compare with that other cowboy, let alone outride him. For the first time that he could remember he was a little nervous as the best, or worst horse in the Morte string was led in the circle of rigs, people and buildings, snubbed, saddled and eased on the kinky back of the bay.

The blindfold was slipped off, and now, if Flint had watched the other rider in surprise that other rider was doing the same in watching Flint. The horse that Flint had chosen for that special occasion was of the kind that's very seldom seen, even amongst the best of the bucking horses. If he made one crooked jump ahead he made three backwards, landing hard and a couple of feet back where he'd leave the earth, not in a backward spin but in side winding, leather-popping jumps that couldn't be looked for, and it was a wonder Flint's double-rig saddle stuck, as for him sticking, well, that was past figuring out. Besides that he quirted and "reefed" (scratched).

But, as it is with people who never rode bucking horses, the hard part of the bay's bucking was missed, and with most of the crowd the ⚵ cowboy had had the hardest horse, because as they looked at it he bucked high and landed hard, where Flint's horse seemed to hardly get off the ground. The stockmen knew that Flint had the hardest horse, but they came to agree with the judges that when it came to points as to really fine and sure riding the ⚵ cowboy had won, without a doubt, for that cowboy had developed his talent into a science, and took the hard jolts as easy as tho the horse had been only loping along. By his riding it was seen that he could of rode Flint's horse better and easier than Flint had, and there's where the decision to his favor came in.

With Flint, as good a ride as he'd done he lacked the really fine points the other rider showed. Flint rode more reckless, careless, and as tho he could do such riding in his sleep. It was just another bucking horse for him, which all he was so used to that he never put a thought to it. And with his natural talent at that it never came to him that with any art there can always be an improvement. The other rider was a "finished" artist at the game where Flint still needed some "polishing."

There was no argument nor hard feelings as to the decision on the winner. Flint only grinned and shook hands with him. But the contest being so close between the two, then the 45 cowboys outriding the others all the way thru, also being decided on that the Morte string was much the worst of the two it was called a "no bet" between the two outfits, and the committee money was divided up equal, so was the prizes, and everybody was satisfied.

But the riding wasn't over, and now that it was settled between the two outfits there was other riders from other outfits who wanted to try their hand. A separate purse had been added on for them, and being that both outfits had brought plenty of horses for the purpose the riding went on till every horse from both outfits was rode, or rode *at*. Not many of the riders who entered their names and was called rode their horse to the finish, especially with the Morte string, but there was a few of them outside cowboys averaged well with the two outfits' top riders, and one or two come mighty close to the winner and Flint as to points.

It was wild riding that went on. Once in a while a blind bucker*
would buck into and break thru the circle of buggies and wagons,
upset and scatter the rigs, along with the lookers-on that might be
in it, and buck on down the main street, sidewalk or any place and
then stampede on. Some of them had to be roped while a rider was
still on 'em, for the pull of the rein on the loose hackamore of a
stampeding outlaw horse to turn him does about as much good as
pulling on his tail.

The bucking horse riding lasted most of the afternoon, and then
as usually happens with such doings and gatherings there was horse
racing. Some of the outsiders and town folks had trained up some
fast horses and now, after some lining up and betting, that went on
to cap the afternoon's doings, far as the doings with horses was
concerned. But there was horse and cow talk as some rejoicing went
on for the rest of the evening. The bars was let down on most
everything, and cowboys, cowmen and town folks all sort of joined
hands and the sky was the limit thru the biggest part of that night.
It was the biggest time that town had ever had and it was sure
making the best of it. All doors wide open, even to the jail house,
for the sheriff and his men was very lenient that night.

While all the pow wows all around was going on and in groups
there was two cowboys who even tho they mixed pretty well with
the crowd stuck mighty close to one another. Them two cowboys
had come to discuss a few things, and after agreeing and deciding
they was seldom seen very far apart that evening.

It was that one of them cowboys had decided to work with the
other. That one was Flint and the other was the 8 rider who'd won

*A horse that don't care how or where he goes.

Some of them had to be roped while a rider was still on 'em.

over him, and the reason for Flint's deciding as to that was to better his riding. His steady and main ambition. But to work together, one or the other would have to quit their outfit and join the other's. The 8 outfit was full handed, but the 45 would welcome another man such as Flint to finish handling the Morte horses.

"Yes," the 8 cowboy had agreed. "I'd like to work with you on that string. I'm about thru with the string I have on hand anyhow and I'll soon be turning them over to work. After that I'll join up with you, if your outfit will still have use for me by then."

"There'll be plenty of use for you, Mark," says Flint, "because there's plenty of rough in them Morte ponies that'll take a long time to get out. I know the outfit sure wants 'em rode so work can be done with 'em, but I have my doubts if that can be done because them ponies seem to be bred with what they got in 'em, never to get out."

So, that's how come that a month later, Mark rode in on the 45 camp with his two private horses, turned 'em free to do nothing but graze with the remuda and went to work with Flint into taking the rough off the worst of the Morte horses.

Them two cowboys had a lot of fun and they wasn't hard on the horses nor in a hurry in taking the rough off 'em. They just pretty well let 'em do as they pleased and just rode 'em, which was sure a plenty by itself. But they also done work with 'em, mostly on "circle" (rounding up the cattle) and at that the foreman was very much satisfied and proud, for the Morte horses was at last getting rode, and rode well.

The only trouble was there was quite a few in that bad Morte strain, twice too many for only two cowboys to keep in working shape and most all of 'em that was turned over to the other cowboys to keep going would soon turn back to their old tricks and Flint and Mark would have to take 'em over again. That was the only trouble the foreman found.

But still he was satisfied, them snorty, kinky bays was at least getting rode, by turns, and even tho a long time between he hoped that them ponies would in time cock their ears with interest to work and not so much with fighting and trying to shake the leather and men that rode 'em.

In the meantime, with his steady riding alongside of Mark, Flint was gradually getting the "polish" he was wanting, and soon enough, with the steady good practice on the tough horses, it was nip and tuck as to which of the two done the best "setting."

A couple of months went by that way, and Mark was about to take his hat off to Flint in recognizing him as the best, when one day the superintendent's two-mule high-wheeled cart rolled into camp. With him was another man, and that other man was out to buy the Morte bunch of outlaws.

The foreman was very much surprised and stumped at hearing of that, and Flint and Mark looked at one another in the same way. "What the samhill," they thought, "would that man want with such horses? Maybe he'd just ship 'em out and sell 'em as unbroke." (Which is often done.)

But they found out soon enough that this man had no such intentions in mind. Far from it. He was willing to pay a top price for the horses, and then the boys and foreman got another big surprise when they was told what them horses was wanted for.

This man, James Hurst by name, was a show man. He'd been with a big Wild West show which at that time was touring the

States, west and east, and even acrost the waters to foreign lands. He'd quit that show, and now that he knew the game and seen what good profits could be made at it he was out to start one of his own.

But he had different ways about starting and as to what his would be. It wasn't going to be no so-called Wild West show. He wouldn't have no Indians chasing stage coaches and cowboys that never seen a cow go a yippeeing and riding little crow-hopping hobby horses, no fancy colored silk shirts nor wild looking show rigs. It'd be no circus and there'd be no paid performers. His idea was to get good tough bucking horses, the tougher the better, then a good bunch of longhorn steers for roping, and the only paid men he'd have would be them to handle the stock with the shipping, feeding and general care of 'em.

With him his shows would go in connection with state and county fairs. His earnings would come from furnishing the stock for such entertainment, either on fixed prices, or gate receipts or both. Then there'd be entry fees which the cowboys would have to pay in order to get in on the bucking horse riding and steer roping, for, as he figured the cowboys who'd come to contest, and that's what he'd make it, a contest, would have to have confidence enough in themselves for a chance to win the good prizes that'd be offered so's they'd be willing to pay fees to enter in the contest. It would be a show for the spectators to pay to see but with the cowboys it would be a serious contest to ride and rope to win one of the prizes, or at least make back what money they'd put in to enter.

With entrance fees that way it would not only eliminate the poorer riders or ropers, but with the better cowboys paying, with their confidence to win a prize, no pay nor nothing else to look

71

forward to if they lost, they would compete so it would also make a better show. It would be a good tough game, each man for himself and a good stake up for the goal. It would be a case, as a contestant once said, where, if "no ride um, no catch um, no eat." In other words it'd be no play nor show with the cowboy.

It took Flint and Mark some time to understand all of that, that they'd have to pay to ride or rope in order to win a prize, so the Hurst man went to explaining some more, that the entrance fees would be small as compared to the prizes that'd be put up, that that money along with the gate money and other money that'd be furnished by the town's clubs, business houses that'd profit and such like would all go to make the prizes bigger, and of course there'd be the stock, the care and shipping of it, capital invested, and there must also be some profit for the man who was promoting such doings, along with the responsibilities of the stock and making the contests good ones for the cowboys, good purses, and good shows for the spectators.

After digesting all of that Flint and Mark seen that Hurst had a good idea, and that a good cowboy could well afford to pay his transportation, expenses, and entrance fees to contest wherever and whenever there was such contests, if the prize moneys was big enough and the cowboy was good enough and believed in his ability to win a prize, or at least break even.

Hurst would call these doings Contests, Cowboy contests, and he already had a few towns sold on the idea for holiday celebrations, such as for the Fourth of July, Labor day, and a couple in between in connection with some fairs further to the East. He seen to it that the papers would be glad to cooperate, announce and advertise the "novel entertainment." Then he'd have folders to send out thru the cow countries telling of the contests, explaining the doings and inviting good cowboys to come and attend and compete.

He wasn't going at it blind, and now all he wanted was good tough stock. He'd seen the Morte horses perform at the stockmen's convention in the Border town, he'd heard about them horses before, and now he was satisfied that he couldn't find no better horses for his purpose anywhere.

So, seeing there wasn't much hopes of them horses ever breaking so good work could be got out of 'em, and Hurst offering a good price, the superintendent decided to let 'em go, let 'em go to a work they was fit for, to bucking and fighting to their hearts' content.

Flint knew the horses that'd be good and could be relied on for the purpose, over half of 'em was out on the horse range. Him and Mark was sent out to round 'em up, cut out the best ones in the corrals there and then bring 'em all, along with the strings they was now working on, to the home ranch, where the deal would be made.

It was a day's ride to the horse range, but right after the noon meal that day the two started out, leading a horse packed with grub and bed. They would gather the horses on the next day, and the two rode on silent and deep in thoughts for a ways, till well away from camp, then Flint finally had to remark.

"Well," he says, "it looks like we're out of a job with this outfit."

"Yep," Mark agreed. "Sold the horses plum out from under us, and we're sure enough afoot here now."

V

ALL GATHERED TO WIN

CLOSE TO TWENTY head of fine big snorty bays was separated from the horse range bunches, all fat and slick as seals, and now, with Flint's and Mark's strings that was picked up at camp on the way to the home ranch that made near forty head of as pretty and tough a bucking string as any man in the contest could wish for, and all good for at least ten years of good hard bucking. They'd be rode, or rode at no more than a couple of times a month, at contests, and all they'd have to do in between times would be to graze on the tall feed they'd be sure to get always, for they'd have to be kept in the best of shape, like with race horses, only they wouldn't have to go thru any hard training as the race horse gets. The only training they'd need would be to be left alone in the grassy rough hills, they'd do the rest whenever they would be run in and caught to be rode.

Hurst was very much pleased with every one of the horses. They didn't have to be tried out, and the superintendent made it plain that he'd be glad to buy back any of the horses that didn't do a satisfactory job of bucking, or any that decided to quit, for he hated to part with them horses, even just as they was.

It was up to Flint and Mark to take the horses to the closest railroad, which was the Border town, and load them to be shipped to another state where Hurst had his ranch and made his headquarters.

They wouldn't be starting with them until the next day, and that night, before the boys took their boots off and crawled under their tarps they come to a final decision on what they'd been discussing while gathering the horses and bringing them in from the horse range that they would now quit the 45 and go on to that neighboring state where the Morte string would be going, and enter in whatever contest where they'd be used, figuring they'd have at least as good a chance to win on the prizes as any of the other contestants. The 45 wouldn't have no more use for them in their particular line of riding anyhow, and this following the contests whenever they come would be something mighty new. They could also get work in between contests with some other outfits on some other rough strings, for there was always plenty of 'em with every good sized outfit.

With that in mind, both Flint and Mark had throwed their private horses, bed and belongings packed on one to each with the Morte horses. From that the foreman took it that they wouldn't be back and he didn't say anything to them about returning, for he knew they didn't want to be just plain good cowhands, and even tho there was still plenty rough horses in every string in the remuda, each string was being rode well and had to be kept that intact. There was no more thru and thru rough string, so when the boys was ready to leave the camp he handed 'em each a slip of their time, the superintendent would make out the check, and all he had to say as they left was that he was sure glad to've had them and there'd be a job for 'em with him whenever they wanted to come back.

It made it easy for them at the home ranch the next morning when, after they drawed their checks from the superintendent and

Hurst got to know about it, he offered 'em the job of taking care of the horses, shipping and all the way thru and delivering 'em to his ranch at the other end. There'd be plenty of room in the cars, he said, and they could load their private horses right in with the others and take 'em along if they wished.

The Morte horses was driven slow to the railroad, taking three days, there was one day on the stock train to the neighboring state and unloading point, and two more days of trailing to the Hurst ranch, a good year around horse country, rough and rocky but with plenty of strong bunch grass, shade, shelter and spring waters. No better place for the Morte string to stay solid in flesh and ornery wild in spirit.

With the horses delivered on that range, all in as good a shape as they was before leaving the 45 range, the boys figured they was thru, for there would be no more caring for their ponies. But no, they wasn't thru yet, Hurst wanted 'em to go out and gather him about forty head of good longhorn steers, and to oblige the boys agreed to do it. In return for the favor, and besides paying 'em good wages, Hurst told 'em he would enter 'em free of charge at his first contest, which date was set to a couple of months off, on a Fourth of July celebration and at a town not so far away where there was a race track and grandstand that could be used.

It didn't take but a little over a week for the boys to get the steers they wanted. Mark had rode in that country before and for one big outfit not so far from the Hurst ranch, and there, amongst the thousands of longhorns and half breeds that roamed the range, him and Flint had no trouble picking out a most likely wild bunch of 'em, of all colors, from pure white to speckled, spotted, brindled,

The Morte horses was driven slow to the railroad, taking three days.

buckskin, red, blue and blacks. Hurst was more than pleased at the sight of 'em, for they wasn't only wild and full of fight but also a mighty showy bunch.

But the boys done more than get the steers while with that big outfit, they each got a job with more spoiled and rough horses, also some unbroken ones, and they was told that these rough ones was so they was pretty well past handling and had been let go one by one till now there was quite a bunch of 'em, enough for two good strings or at least fourteen to each. If they wanted to handle 'em they'd be welcome, and at top wages.

So, talking it over with Hurst, and knowing that he didn't want the Morte string rode, only, as he said, if any it would be by poor hands that couldn't handle 'em and so they'd stay spoiled, and seeing that he had all the hands he needed and there was no more they could do for him they saddled and packed their private horses and rode away, promising Hurst they'd sure be at his first contest on the Fourth, and get what other cowboys they could to come along, for the more come the better the contest and the better the show, said Hurst.

With the Slash A —A, the big outfit, the boys was glad to again be in the thick of the rough ones, for it'd been quite a spell since they'd pulled their saddles off the kinky backs of the Morte horses, and with riding their own horses which was more or less gentle and dependable, shipping, gathering the steers and so on they wasn't only a little leary of getting stale but they missed the action. Besides, with handling and riding the rough ones it's a good idea to keep at it steady to be good and not have anything to do with the gentler horses, for the gentler kind is apt to make a man get careless, and that don't go well when he gets back to the rough ones again.

Flint and Mark found the —A horses plenty rough, and as the foreman had said, pretty well past handling. These picked spoiled ones was again different from the Morte horses, they was much harder to handle from the ground, like with slipping the hackamore on 'em when caught, saddling and getting on or off of 'em. But from there on and when it came to riding 'em they was only just good practice for the two cowboys and couldn't compare with the bucking ability of the Morte horses. The boys agreed after a few days at 'em that Hurst was sure lucky to find such a string, they was natural born buckers. The boys saved their strength and action mostly for that.

"I think," Flint said one day, laughing, "that we better go take a few sittings at them Morte horses before the contest comes off. We're not getting any better on *these* horses."

"No, we ain't" agrees Mark, "but I know for sure that Hurst don't want us on them horses. He don't want 'em rode, he wants 'em only tried."

So the boys had to content themselves with the roughest the —A had, and to keep their job and in practice until the Fourth, for the contest, they took their time in taming 'em down so regular range work could be got out of 'em. But even at that, and in a month's time the foreman seen that half of 'em would do to scatter amongst the cowboys. Flint and Mark was handed a few more next to the roughest to make up their strings, and now they had to go with the regular work, and instead of riding one horse a half hour till all their horses was rode once every day, they changed horses only three times a day and along with the regular cow work, and they now got to riding their horses in turn, which came every three or four days for from three to five hours to each. There was a horse for the morning's circle which sometimes took till middle afternoon, a fresh one to hold the herd while branding or cutting out went on, then maybe another one to stand dayherd shift in the evening. As was with some outfits, the rough string rider also had to stand night guard, which meant another horse. It was seldom a manada or main herd was kept in that country only sometimes during spring and fall, but with the —A outfit there was on an average of three changes of horses a day, and sometimes four, along with that country's way of working.

With the longer times between rides, Flint's and Mark's rough strings kept pretty rough, and even tho it wasn't to the two cowboys' liking and sometimes short on action to be holding herd, standing night guard and the likes they made the best of it and would hold on until a few days before the Fourth. It helped some when a couple of weeks before then, the foreman told 'em they could go back to the camp where they'd been taming the rough ones and gather in a bunch of colts to start in breaking. Him and a couple of other riders went along to help with the gathering, the foreman picked out a nice bunch of four and five year old geldings and the boys was happy again. But before the foreman left 'em at their work they let him know that they'd be hitting out for the contest on the Fourth.

At that the foreman's ears perked up. "Contest?" he asks; "what contest, what kind of contest?"

Flint and Mark explained it all to him.

"Well," he says, surprised, "I never heard of such a thing. Sounds as tho it sure ought to be worth seeing." He stopped, like to ponder a while, and then, "Boys," he says, with a meaning grin, "this outfit will have to be represented at them doings. The work is not going to be so rushing at that time, and with you two boys and some more good riders I have that'll sure want to go I know we're safe to win the bucking horses prizes, then you know I've got some good ropers, so we might win that too, and if we did win on both doings," the foreman's glint lit up more, "why, it'd be more than one feather in the —A outfit's hat but a whole war bonnet."

That was more than agreeable with the outfit all around, and the foreman now allowed the boys to ride as they pleased and made it plain to 'em that he would drop the old rule which was with every well run outfit, that was not to scratch ahead of the cinch when a horse bucked and encourage him that way. That part of the shoulders, *"belonged to the company."* Back of the cinch *"belonged to the cowboy."*

He dropped the old rule on unnecessary roping of big stuff too, and now the boys didn't have to be out of sight of him to unlimber their ropes and roping arms.

But it was understood that that freedom would be allowed only to the time of the contest, and after the contest it'd be back to the old standing rules and work. (It wasn't many years afterwards, when contests got more numerous, and the newness wore off that no more such freedom was allowed by the outfits, and a cowboy was lucky if he could get a few days off to go to a contest without he just quit.)

The work was wild and reckless with the —A outfit during that two weeks up to the Fourth, and not only with that outfit, but with many others that received the folder explaining all about the contest, why the entrance fees to be paid by the cowboys, the few rules, that the cowboy contested at his own risk, paid his own transportation and back, also his expenses, and then the prizes was mentioned, in big looking number.

Every outfit took to the spirit and newness of the contest. And the honor of one outfit's cowboys winning was worth a heap more than the prizes offered. So, during the two weeks to the Fourth there was many a big steer got up dazed after being roped and throwed. Many a snorty horse was sort of surprised that he wasn't held up in his bucking, and not only that but encouraged to do his worst, or best.

There was many spills and many roping mix-ups, and when the day before the Fourth come and the cowboys begin drifting in, Hurst was sort of keeping tally on 'em and he was very satisfied. The next morning one of his men who was taking care of the stock told him he counted over two hundred of the boys. They'd come to the corrals to size the stock up.

"And they sure look like they'd make old Satan hunt a hole if they started anything, on anything."

The corrals, only two of 'em, had been built in the center of the race track field. In one was the Morte string of outlaws, and adjoining in the other corral was the wild-eyed longhorn steers. Them corrals was of good size with filled hay mangers and water troughs in 'em, and Hurst was satisfied again as he looked at his stock on the morning of the Fourth that if there was going to be any falls with the show, it wouldn't be on account of his stock, nor of any of the cowboys present.

Flint and Mark didn't bother much about looking at the stock, for they knew every hoof, hair and horn of 'em. They came to the

In the other corral—was the wild-eyed longhorn steers.

corrals most to mix with the competing riders and see who all was there that they might know. Also to say "How" to Hurst, only to be thanked for what they'd done for him, with horses, cattle, bringing in the —A boys.

Hurst didn't care who won the first, second or third prizes, so long as there was enough contestants to make his first show a good one. There was plenty enough contestants, and even tho he knew that Flint and Mark knew every jump and twist the Morte horses made it was all right by him, for he figured they could ride any bad horse they'd never seen just as well.

Noon come, and before that time the cowboys who wanted to contest put down their names and paid their entrance fees. There was no drawing out of a hat as to which horse a cowboy was to ride, it was to be just as the horses come. Besides it would of been hard to name that Morte string, on account of their looking so all alike.

They'd have to be painted on the hip with big numbers, and then, there was no use of doing that, for any horse that a cowboy slid onto from that string would be sure to make it mighty interesting. They bucked different from one to another but just about as hard to set in each their own way.

Two hundred and fifty cowboys was by the corrals early that afternoon. Most of 'em was entered, paid their fees, and the ones that hadn't, a few of the best old hands that was still curious of what it was all about, was put on the catching and snubbing the Morte horses as they was needed.

With the Fourth of July spirit which started on the afternoon before as range and neighboring town folks drove, rode and mixed in there was quite a crowd to witness the doings, and the track's grandstand represented many states, from "Duck" breeches to broadcloth and from silk tops to plain broad brimmed felt hats. Mayors, senators, and others in such public standing was there with families and friends, Rancheros from south of the line, and below, in the field in the center of the race track, and in one of the two corrals was the Morte string which the people had heard so much of and come to see perform, also the cowboys that was to compete on 'em, cowboys from all parts of the Southwest, with their outfits' owner or superintendent witnessing and betting on them. There'd be no old fashioned baseball game on that Fourth.

VI

THE MORTE STRING

A LITTLE TOWN band played a lively tune from the center of the grandstand and then afterwards Hurst himself took up a megaphone and went on to explaining to the crowd all about the contest, how about the cowboys being of the best and that the goings on wouldn't be just riding the bucking horses just for the fun of it or for show. It wouldn't be no Wild West circus or exhibition, that no cowboys would be getting any pay only from the prizes they might win. It would be a hard fought contest all the way thru, the same with the steer roping. Hurst told of the few simple rules and then the origin and story of the Morte horses which was to furnish the action in the bucking horse contest. He wasn't backward in saying that they was the best in bucking ability and the worst outlaws in the whole Southwest. He told of how only a couple of cowboys had been able to ride 'em. That'd been for just a short time, after years of wild freedom for them horses. But they was still as wicked as ever, if not more so, for there was no taking the outlaw out of 'em.

He told quite a story about the longhorn steers too, that they'd been picked out of thousands of head of their kind and would sure make the ropes sing and pop in the roping contest.

His talk over with, the band played another tune while most of the cowboys rode in on a short parade or grand entree in front of

The town mayor rode in the lead.

the grandstand, the town mayor rode in the lead, a cowboy bearing the American flag and the rest following behind on whatever horses had been brought along or dug up for that purpose. After that, and with a sign from Hurst, the judges, snubbers and pick up men rode to their right places and the first Morte horse was roped and led out of the corral to be snubbed as a cowboy's name was called that was to saddle and straddle him. The contest was started.

The Morte bays didn't disappoint the crowd, nor Hurst, for as the blindfold was slipped off one after another and they lowered their heads to their crooked hard bucking there was no more could be asked as to the action they put on, and as six of the first horses had done their stuff, only one of the six riders put up a qualifying ride—loosened bad thru that ride but he didn't touch the nubbin (grab the horn) and he did do a little quirting. Two others rode all over their horses and grabbed everything they could get a hold of from hooking the cinch to grabbing saddle strings and the horn. They stayed on their horses till picked up but being they didn't ride according to the rules their names was scratched off the list. The three other riders couldn't set up with the earth jarring bucks, and after considerable hard trying had to skeedaddle out of their saddles to meet up with their shadows on the ground.

With such goings on most of the rest of the boys that was to be called to follow on in trying to put up a ride on the hurricane deck of such horses felt sort of nervous in seeing it would be pretty hopeless. With that feeling, a few was as well as bucked off before they straddled their horses.

There was no contradicting that the Morte string was the most wicked that'd ever been seen. That was well agreed on, not only amongst the riders but with people who didn't have to try and ride 'em, the people in the grandstand.

The Morte string more than lived up to what Hurst had said about 'em. Out of eight of 'em, only four riders stuck and only two made halfways qualifying rides so their names was kept off the list. But to match up with that there was two of the boys had to be taken to the hospital, one who'd got bucked off and kicked before he hit the ground, smashing a few ribs, and another with a broken leg as he'd bounced after hitting the ground and the horse going over him took one of the rider's legs down into the ground with a hard landing front hoof.

Such goings on was new to the spectators, and even tho there was often such happenings with work on the range it didn't quite go with the Fourth of July's spirit and celebration. Hurst kind of felt as to how the crowd might look at it, and so, seeing it was time a good ride was brought on, for a sort of free breathing and relieving spell, Mark was called as a next rider, and he was the first rider amongst the riders before him that was announced, as the best of riders on one of the worst of the Morte horses.

The crowd cheered, and as Mark slipped into the saddle, smiling and looking so confident, they figured that here would be a ride, and right then the crowd, sort of getting used to the doings, and as all crowds do in wanting thrills and hollering for blood, didn't care if the cowboy broke his neck or the horse crumpled in a heap, it'd sure be worth watching.

It was very much worth watching, but so well done with both the rider and the horse that, over the average of the grandstand, people was a little disappointed. It was their first time to see a top rider on a top bucking horse, and they'd got so, from the rides before, they couldn't see why the rider didn't fall off or the horse didn't break his neck or the rider's neck or something happen.

The cowmen and contesting cowboys was about the only ones who appreciated and thought they'd witnessed where neither rider nor horse could be beat. They hardly believed their sight, and that ride made the judges blink.

Hurst, being the showman he was, seen where the crowd was now satisfied, had got over their first scare, and not only that but was now anxious for more spills and thrills.

The cowmen and contesting cowboys was still dwelling on the good ride Mark had made, for skill and good riding was more pleasing to them. They'd seen the rough side of riding before. But with the average crowd, and Hurst wanting to keep the contest lively, he figured that the riders following would now furnish the thrills for a spell. If that got to be too much with the crowd he still had two good riders he figured would bring their hearts to normal. One of them riders was Flint, and the other was one Hurst had hired to break the Morte string, not letting him know what them horses was, and figuring he'd only get bucked off, keeping the horses in their good bucking habit that way. But that cowboy had surprised him a considerable and only a few of the Morte string got to buck him off. After that Hurst told this cowboy what these horses really was, to which that rider only grinned and remarked "I don't like to be paid breaking wages when I was really stomping out spoiled ones."

To that this cowboy got the proper raise in wages, and being the contest had then been only a few days off he'd been kept on pay till that time, but not to ride them horses no more, only to do the handling and shipping of 'em, as Flint and Mark had done.

With the riders that followed on after Mark's ride, Hurst thought that the change of heart amongst the crowd would now be pleased along with their sudden want of thrills and spills. But it seemed the worst riders had been called first on the list, and now the most of 'em that rode after Mark's fine doings done pretty well, so well that even tho Mark had easy outrode 'em to the judge's opinion there was four or five rode out that'd be sort of hard to decide on as to second after Mark, and the crowd, now sort of used or hardened or thrill hungry, wasn't getting as much fun or excitement as with the first cowboys that piled off (got throwed) and hurt.

Then Hurst's rider, the one he'd hired to "break" the Morte horses, was called. He of course had the advantage of the other riders, excepting Mark, because he'd tried out and knew the horses, but even at that he was the better rider outside of Mark. Even them in the crowd that didn't know and never rode anything rougher than a rocking chair couldn't help but marvel at his riding, and now the judges felt relieved as to which would win second in the bucking horse riding. Mark was of course decided as easy the first.

More cowboys took to the Morte horses and rode well, few made qualifying rides and amongst 'em that did none could come up to Nat, the Hurst rider, for second; much less to Mark. It was well seen and admitted by the visiting cowmen and contesting cowboys that no such a bunch of horses had ever been witnessed to or met up with as the Morte string. It was no disgrace to be bucked off any of 'em, for that could happen even with very good and above ordinary riders.

Over thirty of the Morte horses was rode or rode at. Not a one of 'em got spooked to stampeding or didn't do their good job of bucking, not a one was easy and not a one fell. Only some bluffed at falling backwards, which made the riders loosen and most always get bucked off as the horse whirled to a stiff, crooked and unlooked for, and an impossible jolt to take if loosened from the saddle a bit.

All the riders, all but one, that'd entered in the bucking horse contest had been called, done their best, and the judges was sure as to their men, without any doubt, for first and second in the prizes. They was still debating some as to the third prize and which one amongst the many good riders that had contested so close for that third prize. But there was that one last rider, and they'd wait till he done his riding before they'd do the final deciding.

There was still quite a few of the Morte horses that hadn't been used, and with this last rider on the list, Hurst once again picked up his megaphone. The way he introduced and announced this rider it was like his big punch to a good bucking horse contest, which it had been all the way thru, and the crowd all perked up some more in expecting. Then Flint was called as another snaky Morte bay was led in.

The crowd, even the most ignorant among it, wasn't disappointed in all they expected in Flint's ride nor the kind of a horse he rode. Such a ride as was witnessed made even many of the good cowboy contestants gawk, and now, after it was over the judges got their noses down their lists and was no more doubtful as they had been as to the winner of the third prize, only they had to make one jump ahead, and now it was well decided and agreeable amongst all the three judges that Flint was first prize winner, Mark second, and Nat third.

That was announced to the crowd amongst a lot of cheer. The visiting cowmen also cheered and agreed, and the contesting cowboys figured it was sure right. It was seldom they'd ever seen such riding, and never before such horses as that string of Morte bays.

After the bucking horse contest was over, Mark came over to Flint and with a long grin stuck out his paw and the two shook hands.

"You was the only one I was afraid of to outride me," says Mark, "and I had good reason to be. But it's sure no shame to come second to you, Flint. You sure done a bear of a ride."

That evening, after the roping contest and all was over and Hurst hid out to count up the money received, and he finally come out apurring and gave the winners their prize money, he tried to make 'em feel that he was more than fair in the money he awarded 'em, but was glad to do it on account of the good "performance" they'd done.

Flint received seventy five dollars for first prize in the bucking horse riding, Mark received sixty and Nat thirty five.

The boys, considering the crowd that had attended, besides other moneys Hurst would get, figured them prizes as mighty small as to what Hurst had raked in, but there was nothing could be done about it, and the boys that didn't win anything, had got tossed and some of 'em badly hurt and a long ways from their home range, had to of course make out the best they could. There was nothing coming to them. But that was all in the game and as had been made understood.

Flint and Mark didn't get anywheres as to winning any prize with the steer roping, Nat managed to get in on third but had to split the money with another cowboy who'd tied with him to the second.

All the way thru the steer roping was, in its own way, near as full of action, spills and thrills as with the bucking horse contest. These steers was anything but of the barn yard kind, they came out at the speed of a good horse for a ways, and when they hit the end of the rope at that speed something was sure to pop. Most of the time the steers done the popping and was upended to lay long enough to be tied. When they didn't pop something else would be sure to. It would be the rope, even sometimes a saddle horn snapped off, or saddle cinchas as the whole rig, cowboy and all was jerked off his horse. If the whale line held, the horse would be jerked down, sometimes straight over backwards. There was mixups too that more than satisfied the crowd for excitement and of the kind that very few of 'em had ever witnessed before, none ever in front of a grandstand and as a contest. They'd had more than their money's worth.

Hurst showed his showmanship when, a while before the crowd got to expecting the end of the steer roping and thinking of filing out, he made a big announcement of another contest he was going to put on at some other town a couple of hundred miles away and at a good date along with a county fair that was a month off. There'd be some more good riders and ropers there and he'd have special extra entertainments with the contest. The admission would be the same and all was invited to attend, and so on. He then introduced the champion riders and ropers of the day and that all went well.

It also went well with Flint and Mark, for even tho they could of gone back to the —A and went on with breaking horses, they met up with the superintendent of another outfit, the "Double Rafter" (∿) whose main ranch was to within only a day's ride of the town where Hurst was going to hold his next rodeo. They'd be located at that main ranch, and another good part of it was that they wouldn't be just breaking young horses but they'd be handed a good bunch of spoiled ones again, the superintendent hoping that some of them could be lined out to work, they was good sized horses and of good age.

Well, that of course struck the two cowboys fine, and it wasn't but a few days when they rode in on the ∿, turned their private horses loose and went to work on the rough ones there.

The months to the fair and contest date went well and peaceful with the boys. These ponies was plenty tough, tougher than the ─A rough ones had been, and even tho few got to be of much use for range work, the boys got plenty of practice and by the time the contest came on they was fit for any tough horse wether he'd be devil or man raised.

There was good men, and many came from long distances to this second contest, for by that time the news of the first contest had spread far and wide in the range country. But Flint again won first prize easy enough in the bucking horse contest, and even tho Mark had to ride mighty close, he got the second. But Nat didn't have no chance for third and had to content himself with second on roping. It was agreed by the three that they'd met up with as good a bunch of cowboys as they'd ever seen.

"Yes," Flint added on, "and with the contests going on there'll still be better ones. We better get down to real riding."

It was near at the end of that contest when Hurst announced that there'd be another contest in some bigger town on Labor Day, with still more attractions along with it.

"Why, that's just a few weeks off," says Mark. "We better get back to the outfit and get to work some more, and harder."

Hurst made much better money at this second contest and the winners received little better prizes, which was encouraging.

Flint and Mark had again been hard at it on the slippery backs of the 〜 horses for some days when to their surprise a rider comes along. It was Nat, and with a two leaf folder telling of a contest. It wasn't a Hurst folder but of another contest being put on, by a man named Randall. This man Randall would be putting on a bigger contest, in a bigger town and at the same date Hurst would, on Labor Day.

"Well," says Mark after digesting the surprising news. "It looks like that now it's going to be contests contesting against contests. This Randall feller is sure offering better prizes than Hurst is."

The boys looked at one another for a spell and then Flint says, "As I get to thinking it might be a good idea to try this new outfit. That town is no further than where Hurst is going to be and I'd like to see how tough a string of horses he's got. I'd bet a good hat they're just pets as compared to the Morte string."

Nat's eyes brightened up at that thought, for the Morte horses had been pretty tough on him and he figured that with this Randall string he'd be pretty sure to come in on third prize. He couldn't hoped for first nor second, not if Flint and Mark rode there. But he says:

"I think it would be a good idea if we all three went to try out them Randall horses. He at least offers better prizes anyway. And boys," he went on, "it'd sure be fine if I could sort of prime up with yez by getting a job riding along on some of these ∿ horses."

"Well I guess that can be easy enough fixed because there's plenty of 'em here that we haven't got to yet."

It was easy enough fixed, and the next day, Nat went to work in the corrals with Flint and Mark. He found the snaky ∿ pretty hard to set and he didn't dare loosen up and he didn't get to do much of "the pretty" riding that goes so well with the judges and towards winning a prize. But that was the kind of practice he wanted, to make him a better rider. Nat was older than Mark, near thirty, and he didn't realize or wouldn't let himself realize that he'd some years before reached his peak at riding the rough ones. He was still on that peak and well above most riders but he couldn't get no better, if anything he'd soon enough *have* to realize that he had done his best riding. The steady "fighting" (handling and riding) of the rough string had left many marks on him, inside and out, and with that accumulating it wasn't so far away when that'd pile up on him, and there he'd be riding downhill to gentler ones.

But even tho more careful, he was still at his usual best while with Flint and Mark in the ∿ corrals, and as he rode outlaw after outlaw each day he got to thinking he was doing better and got anxious for the Labor Day doings to come.

All the while, Flint was again thinking he was getting stale, for he'd got so used to the tough ones that even while the worst was doing their worst he'd sometimes be thinking of that last plate of ham and eggs while in town, the pretty waitress, or some such other things plum away from his "work."

As things was thought and talked over off and on about the two contests coming on the same day, Flint and Mark finally come to an idea which they decided was sure a good one. It was that they split, Mark to go to the Hurst contest. He'd be about sure to win the first, being Flint wouldn't be contesting there, and Flint was to go to the Randall contest, and that way both would be more than likely to get their first prizes.

Nat agreed that would be a very good idea too, for that'd now give him a good chance to get second instead of third prize as he'd been getting.

"I got to be satisfied with the leavings when you two are contesting," he grinned, "and I'll have more chance when I buck up against one of you instead of two."

And thinking of the Morte horses, Nat went on to say: "I think I'll go with Flint. I know I'll have more chance on Randall's horses than I would on Hurst's and maybe put up a real ride, but with them Morte horses I feel mighty lucky to just stay on top and leave the leather alone. Besides I can't expect more than second anyhow in whichever contest I take, and I'd just as well make it easy on myself."

So, that's how come that when Labor Day come and it was near time for the contests to start that afternoon, Flint and Nat was at Randall's corrals sizing up the horses and riders and Mark was at Hurst's corrals, not looking at the horses, for he knew every one of them well. What he was sizing up the most under his hat brim was the riders, and he was pleased to feel that he needn't fear any of 'em.

Randall's bigger prizes had drawed most of the best, and he had to grin and at the same time feel sorry for Flint and Nat because, as he figured, they'd sure have a tough and big gathering of riders to buck up against there. They'd sure have to ride for their money.

But they didn't have to *ride*, that is, Flint didn't. He straddled a big, lanky gray that fought like a wolf and Flint pulled up on his shap belt, thinking sure that here would be *some* horse. He was all pleased about it as he yanked off the blind and "went to work" on him. And then's when he got the surprise of his life, which near caused him to fall off on account of it. It was that he'd expected a real bucking horse when all he got was a very average one, and any unbroken one could of done as well if not better.

He seen where there could be no first prize won on such a horse, and that made Flint see red. He went after that big rawboned gray like he was going to eat him up but there was no use. That horse could buck just so hard and no harder.

Flint didn't wait for no pick up man as the whistle blowed, he just "goosed" (spurred) the big gray close to the ears and let him slip from under him, leaving Flint standing on his feet and raving mad. When he walked past the judges on his way back to the corral, he remarked to 'em, "If that's a bucking horse I'm a lolly-pop."

Flint hit for the shady side of the plank corral and there squatted to let his feelings ease a bit the while he watched on with a disgusted look as horse after horse was led out, snubbed and rode. Some of the horses was pretty good, he thought, but the one he'd rode was, to him, the scrub of the bunch while other contestants thought he'd bucked hard enough. But Flint felt he was now out, all on account of such a poor horse, and that's what hurt.

"If that's a bucking horse, I'm a lolly-pop."

It hurt him so that he finally walked to Randall who looked pleased the way his horses acted, for a few of the poorer riders had been throwed, and he figured he had a sure enough bucking string of tough horses.

So it was some surprise and set back when Flint, still some peeved, came to him and asked if he had any bucking horses in his string, that he'd rode one, watched quite a few others but hadn't seen one *buck* yet. If he had one he'd like to try him, in the contest.

Randall got pretty well peeved at that himself. He just glared at Flint and without saying a word to him told one of the ropers to catch one certain horse which he pointed out. The horse, another big fighter, was led out, the judges was informed that Flint would be riding again for another chance at the prize, and Flint grinned, mighty pleased.

But this big fighting outlaw turned out to be as poor a bucking horse, to Flint's way of thinking, as the gray he'd rode before, and even tho the judges was satisfied that here was a qualifying ride, that cowboy didn't think so, not on such a poor bucking horse as he figured he was on, and he seen red again. He throwed the rein away, stuck both hands high in the air and rode him thru some hard jumps that way. That would of won him the first prize right there, but Flint was only doing that to show his contempt for such bucking stock, and before the whistle blowed, like to throw the horse away, he slid off of him and let him go. That of course disqualified him right there.

Flint was now past being mad. He hardly seen anything or any-body as he walked back to the corral, and he didn't say a word, only the disgusted look he wore told aplenty and made the contestants grin at one another.

Come to the last rider, it was Nat, and at that, Flint's gloomy look turned to one of interest. He hoped Nat would draw a good horse and bring home the bacon. And Nat did draw a good horse, none could of fitted him more, and there was some action put on by both that horse and rider that made the crowd stand and cheer like had never been heard before. That ride sure looked like first prize to Flint and he was mighty pleased.

Then, when he figured that was the last of the bucking contest and he was congratulating Nat on his ride, Randall came to him and says: "You don't seem to think much of my bucking horses," he begins, and before Flint could say anything to that, he went on, "I don't want you to keep thinking that, and so, if you want to try one more I think I've got one that'll please you. You're now disqualified but this ride will put you back in the contest, and if you make a good one on him you can still be up for one of the prizes. Want to try him?"

Flint didn't answer by words, only by such a grateful grin that Randall just turned away and pointed another certain horse for a roper to catch and lead out.

This horse, a good sized rangy bay, didn't fight much as he was led out, snubbed and saddled. His color and actions was more like of the wise Morte horses, saving strength and action for when the blind was pulled off, and even tho Flint didn't know anything about how to pray, this was one time when, with his hopes, no better praying was ever done that this horse would be at least as good as the poorest of the Morte horses. Then he'd have a chance to show his ability to the judges and what riding really was like.

That was the trouble with Flint, the tough, hard to set Morte horses had spoiled him and got his natural ability trained up so fine that it seemed no other horses could really buck.

But with this bay that was led out his interest came to life and his hopes went high. This last and final ride for the contest was announced to the crowd, as to Flint being twice first prize winner at two other contests, and the horse as being the picked best bucking horse and worst outlaw in the Randall string.

Flint was still praying that here would be one of the same kind as the Morte horses as he slipped into the saddle. He'd sure give that horse his head and go after him from the start, and if this wasn't going to be a ride, well . . .

And it was a ride. As the blindfold was slipped off, Flint reached high on the bay's neck and at the same time let out a war whoop that'd put a whole tribe of warring Indians to silence. From there on the wild ride started, the bay let out a choking beller, made one hard jump . . . then hit out in a wild run, stampeded.

The one buck was all that horse done, after that he of a sudden turned out to be a race horse. He jumped over the low railing into the race track and away he went, Randall's best bucking horse.

As tense as the crowd and all had been to see that top bad horse and great rider do some real work, that tenseness had switched to hollers and roars of laughing. Around the track the horse went, like any good race horse, and to keep from walking too far, Flint rode. He rode till the horse got back near the corral and then he goosed him in the neck again, to see if there was any buck in him at all, but the bay just slowed down to crowhop and that was all. So, before he lined out to run some more, Flint goosed him again, and with the crowhop that come he quit him. The horse then was roped by some riders that'd been by the track and ready.

Flint, in being so anxious for the horse to do a good job of bucking, had went after him a little too hard, and what really happened was that he *scared* the buck plum out of him, which started him to running instead, and like to get away from the devil himself.

But if Flint was disappointed he finally had to swallow that and go to laughing with the crowd, especially after looking at Randall who, after such announcing as he'd done about his best bucking horse, acted like he wanted to hunt a hole and dive into it.

There'd be no more horses for Flint, for he seemed to be the Jinx and the bucking horse contest was called to an end. But all the way thru the horses had bucked pretty good and the crowd was satisfied.

The next attraction was a chuck wagon race, but with no chuck in the wagons, only two cowboys and four spooky horses hooked to each wagon. There was three wagons in the race, two of 'em tangled up as the race was on, with the result that there was a front broken wheel on one and the other was turned over, the team going on and dragging it on its side for a ways. A wheeler fell with the third wagon was drug a ways and then broke loose, the three horse team coming in first, and the other wagon with dragging front axle coming in second. The third wagon was put back on its wheels but was too late coming in to be in the race.

All in all the doings was very exciting to the crowd, also to a couple of cowboys who had to do some tall scrambling to keep clear of entanglements and all that came their way.

The steer roping was next. Randall had some good steers but not as good as Hurst had. They didn't have the wiry speed that makes good tough roping. But the crowd and all was satisfied there again, and that ended the day's doings and contest.

Flint didn't enter in the roping, for he knew he wouldn't have no chance against all the good ropers that was there. But Nat was on the job there again, and even tho it was seen he wouldn't be in the prize money at that, this time he done mighty good and quick work in both roping and tying.

Most of the contestants stuck around after all was over, till the judges and Randall summed up the prizes and the winners was decided on. Flint was among 'em, and when the decisions was handed out he was surprised but pleased that Nat had won the first prize in the bucking horse contest. So was Nat, especially when Flint had also been contesting, besides having his chance on three horses.

"But," one of the judges told Flint afterwards, "if you'd of rode on the way you was doing on the second horse, with your hands high and all that we'd of *had* to given you first. But what did you do? Like a durn fool you quit your horse before we blowed the whistle and disqualified yourself, just when you'd about won."

The judge was surprised and wondered when, as he looked and frowned at Flint, that instead of the sorry look he expected to see on his face, that cowboy only had a wide and pleased grin there.

"Well, I'm glad to know I could of won anyway," he says.

It had hurt him pretty deep that he couldn't be first, for he hadn't took to losing as yet and the first time always goes pretty hard. But now, with the judge's explaining he felt some better, and he was glad it was Nat who'd won the first prize.

Mark, with the Hurst string, didn't have so much trouble riding off with the first prize there, and now the tables was sort of turned, for Mark and Nat having been second and third after Flint, was now both first prize winners, and Flint didn't even make third.

But that was all very well understood amongst the three, and as they gathered again at the ∿ main camp, Mark had some tall news to tell. Hurst had got peeved at Randall for putting on his contest on the same day, drawing away some of the crowd, and most of the best cowboys by offering bigger prizes. That didn't help his contest any, and now he'd decided to take a couple of months' time, turn his horses and steers out on his range to stock up on good hard fat, figure out a program for a real contest and show, arrange so it could be pulled off in some good big town, and not only for one day but for two days with this next one. Mark didn't know just where this big contest was going to be pulled off but Hurst would let him know in time so he could be on hand, also Flint and Nat, for as he'd said he wanted the best of the cowboys to come and contest on the best of bucking horses, and rope at the wildest of steers. And that wouldn't be all, there'd be other doings he'd brew up for the cowboys to contest and win prizes in during the two months or so he'd be mapping out his program, and the best part of it, as Mark said, was that the prizes would be twice the amount Randall had given. The first prize for bucking horse contest would be two hundred dollars, and near the same for the first in steer roping.

"Well, according to that," Nat finally got to remark, "it'll be some contest worth going to and that'll draw riders that might be able to stomp on them Morte horses pretty well."

"Yep, maybe," says Flint, "but whatever rider goes to stomping on them Morte horses will sure find out they'll have aplenty to stomp."

VII
THE COWBOY CONTESTS ARE ON

I T WAS THREE months and more by the time Hurst got every thing fixed up and his program mapped out for his new "Grand Contest," as he called it, and before that time the three cowboys of the ∽ had pretty well run out of rough ones there. Flint had caught up his private horses and hit out for other territories in search for more rough ones. Mark went his way too, but Nat stayed on to fan out what was left of the ornery ones. They was plenty tough enough for him and he could be kept busy at that for some time yet.

Finding another string of rough ones to work on wasn't so easy, and for a time, Flint had to content himself with just a regular rough string and ride 'em along with the work on the range. Mark had to do the same on another outfit, and even tho regular riding, such as the rounding up of cattle, branding, holding herd and the like wasn't to either of the cowboys' taste, it was sure better than laying idle, and the horses they rode was rough enough to keep 'em in trim.

When the time come for Hurst to put on his Grand Contest and he notified the boys of it, they wondered if they should make it, if with the expense and the time it'd be worth while, for it would be pulled off quite a ways to the east and they'd have to take the train to get there. But after reading the folder and seeing of the many and new goings on, where they might win something besides the bucking horse contest, they finally decided to make it there. With Flint and on them Morte horses he felt pretty sure of winning a prize regardless of what good riders came to contest, and that fact is what made Mark and Nat sort of hesitate to go, for, with Flint contesting they knew they couldn't expect more than second or third, but there again and with the other goings on where they might win, they figured they could at least break even and make expenses. Besides it was figured that this new big contest would sure be worth seeing.

So, that's how come the three cowboys was present and gathered again on the evening before the first day of the contest, and all the number of cowboys that came in at Hurst's office and was scattered thru the big town, was the biggest gathering of the bow-legged gentry they'd ever seen at one time. These riders was from all parts of the western ranges, quite a few from Mexico and even a sprinkling from the wide plains of western Canada.

The opening of the contest the first afternoon was started with loud tunes from a good band as the contestants rode thru a parade in front of the crowded grandstand. Then the bucking horse contest was on, while the band played some more off and on. There was a cowboy clown too, dressed as a hayseed, with whiskers, straw hat and all the trimmings, even to the big red bandanna hanging down from his hip pocket, corn cob pipe, and packing a carpet bag which he pulled some laughing tricks out of. The crowd in the grandstand thought he was a sure enough hick from the

*The crowd in the grandstand thought he was a sure enough hick
from the farm, but he was all cowboy and a good one.*

farm, but he was all cowboy and a good one, and the crowd was kept surprised and laughing with the tricks he done, which was sure good from what they thought was only a hick hayseed.

He done his clowning with rope and big six shooter during the times the bucking horses was getting snubbed and saddled, along while the band played, and the crowd was some surprised when he came out on a bucking horse himself, not a Morte horse, riding him backwards and bareback, with just a rope around his middle and fanning him with his carpet bag. At a certain time the bag came open and a big red rooster flew out. Then he quit his horse and went around and around after that rooster, which was trained, would wait till the clown got to within a few feet of him and then start running again. The clown shot blank cartridges at him, finally roped him and put him back in his carpet bag, amongst some red underwear and other dirty clothes he had in there to exhibit with his act. Outside of the men handling the stock and the judges, the clown was the only one on salary with the contest.

The Morte horses came out true to their reputation. Hurst changed the rules some, and at the request of some humane folks who didn't understand the quirting was barred, the rider could fan only with his hat, then the spur rowels had to be taped, for them same folks thought them big rowels to be mighty wicked and was gauged into a horse plum to the hilt or shank. The truth is they wasn't near as cruel as the little sharp pointed rowels of them times. Another rule, and to make it harder on the riders, was that only one rein was to be used on the bucking horses, whereas before the regular two had been used, as on the range.

But the contest went on in great style, and with the clown and the band keeping things going there was no dragging spells. The crowd enjoyed it all to the limit.

Flint drawed a horse to his taste, done a powerful good ride and it looked like first prize for him. Mark had the hard luck of getting bucked off. He'd rode too wild, got too reckless and now, with his getting bucked off as the result, he was plum out of the bucking contest. Nat done a fair ride, but being the Morte horses was a little too much for him it looked doubtful if he'd be in even on third prize, for there was many top riders there for that big two day contest. Two of them was hurt pretty bad and was carted to the hospital and one come near getting killed as he was throwed, his foot catching in the stirrup and the spur in the cinch. He was dragged quite a ways before he was kicked loose, caving in some ribs on him and breaking an arm.

The next doings or event was the stake race, where about ten cowboys on the best cowhorses that could be dug up raced five hundred yards each to a stake in the ground, turned sharp as they could around each stake and raced back to the starting ground.

Then came the steer roping where there was some good and fast work done and some pretty wild mixups happened. Nat was in on that as usual, and Mark tried his luck too, doing pretty good time.

After that, came an event that was all new, not only to the folks in the grandstand but also to most of the cowboys. It was where two cowboys rode alongside a steer, one jumped off his horse, landed on the steer's neck, grabbing both horns, then the neck was twisted and the steer was throwed while running at full speed. That fast and new way of throwing a steer got to be called "hoolihan" and the event "bull dogging."

The humane society put a stop to the hoolihan way of throwing a steer on account it was figured as cruel, and nowdays the steer has to be brought to a stop before throwing, and that's not so easy done even by the cowboys who know how. The name "bull dogging" was changed to steer wrassling. That sounded less wicked, besides, with "bull dogging," some folks got the idea that it was where a steer was turned into an arena and a bunch of bull dogs was turned loose on him to get him down.

Being that was the first of such doings only four cowboys contested in that. They was mostly Oklahoma boys, and the decision as to the winners for that was the same as with roping, all as to the length of time it took for the bull dogger to get his steer down flat and to holding him still for a couple of seconds.

That was quite a thrill to the crowd and all present. But the next event that followed was still better, it was a wild horse race. That town was quite a horse market center, there was a good many unbroke range and wild horses in the yards that'd been shipped in from the western ranges and was to be put on auction sale, and for a small sum Hurst had rented about twenty of 'em for that purpose. None of the wild ones was broke even to lead, and as each was roped and manouvered out of the corral one cowboy would grab for a hold of his ears, twist 'em and do his best to hold the horse to a standstill that way till another cowboy slipped a rope halter and gunnysack blind on him.

The saddling wasn't to start until every horse was out and each man had his, and the commotion that was stirred as horse after horse was got out of the corral often scattered cowboys and the horses already caught and being held until time for all to start saddling.

The horses was brought out in fast enough time and each handed to two cowboys, one to help handle and hold the wild one and the other to do the saddling and ride him in the race. All the horses out, the whistle blowed for every rider to go to saddling, and then, to get that done in as fast a time as possible there was another commotion, and many a horse run into another, sometimes three or four tangled up in one mixup, horses jumping over, going under or right into others, saddles being bucked or jerked off before they was cinched and every cowboy hanging on to his horse for all he was worth.

Horses jumping over, going over or right into others, saddles being bucked or jerked off before they was cinched.

There was no standing starting point in the race, the race was started from the time the whistle blowed to go to saddling, and the first man saddled, on his way past the grandstand and to a point a few hundred yards beyond it, would be the winner. The race was to be on the track, but with these unbroken wild horses the track was too narrow for most of 'em and the railing between the track and the field inside it was bucked into and thru.

That race was a sure enough wild horse race. It was a great sight to see the twenty wild horses, each being rode for the first time most all abucking or stampeding, running into and sometimes upsetting one another, going all directions and not at all like a regular race, for, of course none of 'em was bridlewise and the only way a cowboy could try to get 'em to go where he wanted 'em to was with spooking 'em by holding his hat on one side of their head or the other in trying to turn and aiming 'em for the finishing line. Most of the time the wild ones would snort and go to bucking at the sight of the hat appearing alongside of their head, and with only a loose halter on 'em and a one inch rope for the rein, there was no steering 'em that way, for they'd never felt a rein on their neck and like any wild animal, deer or antelope they'd never been turned by any human atop of 'em before.

One of the wild ones finally left the mixup of buckers and spinners and hit out like a scared rabbit, stampeding for the finishing line and doing a very good job for speed. The cowboy riding him was sure of winning and kept adusting that wild one's rump with his hat to keep him going. The horse went on full speed ahead and the finishing line was only a few yards ahead when that pony, for no reason that could be accounted for, of a sudden bogged his head, whirled and went to bucking, and when he straightened up from that he lit into stampeding again just as fast as before, and now right back to the whirling and bucking wild bunch which now was beginning to scatter and hitting out for all directions excepting towards the finishing line in the track.

Finally, one more cowboy, after taking the first buck out of his horse, got to hazing out with his hat and headed the right direction, by jerks, and he had him close to the line, with a good chance to win, when of a sudden another stampeding horse came by and passed him like a streak, just when that cowboy figured he'd about won the race.

The wild horse race is always a great wind-up event to any contest and sure puts the cap on all the other good events that comes before it. I've never seen no crowd that didn't more than enjoy that.

There was prizes or "day money" given for all events for that first day, all excepting for bucking horse riding, that would be handed out on the next day, when some of the riders who had qualified would have to ride and compete again for a final decision. So many had entered in that event that they hadn't all got to ride on the first day. They would all get to ride on the second day, that would be a tryout for the rest of the riders, only a few of them who'd broke the first day had qualified for the final contest, they'd be competing along with the others that would qualify on the next day.

Flint had of course qualified and well, and so was listed to ride again on the final ride the next day. Mark was out of it altogether and didn't feel so good about it. But Nat made it and had hopes for at least third in the winnings.

The next day being Sunday and the people and *Daily News* making so much fuss as to how good and exciting the contest had been the day before, there was quite some crowd in the grandstand, which was filled, and even standing room was scarce. Looked like the whole town was there to see the second and last day of the "Grand Contest." There was no busier nor more pleased man than Hurst was on that sunny Saturday.

The goings on was about the same as the day before. It couldn't of been any better, only the cowboys had the rough end of it and a few more was laid up, but that was all in the game and taken as it come.

But Flint never rode better than he did in the final contest that was to decide on the prizes, and with the good reliable, hard bucking Morte horse that was tearing up the earth under him there was no hesitation amongst the judges when it come time to award him the first prize in the bucking contest.

Poor Nat didn't have a chance in that final contest. He rode his horse all right but he done too close and safe a ride and quite a few of the other final contestants outrode him. He didn't get to make even third prize.

But he sort of made up for that in steer roping, worked mighty fast and won third prize there, by two seconds.

Mark also tried his hand there but he was quite a few seconds slow of even the third prize. But to half way square things up, and luck being with him, he won the wild horse race, twenty five dollars, "and that's better than nothing" he grinned to Flint and Nat afterwards.

Better than nothing was right, for many of the boys not only hadn't won anything but they'd come a long ways, was out quite an expense and considerable time, and some was wondering how to get back. Then there was others laying in the hospitals, some would be there quite a while, months afterwards, before they would be able to ride and do regular range work again, most of 'em with their saddles in hock and broke to boot.

But that's not considered nor thought of by the crowds that come to watch a contest, to them a spill is a thrill. But there again and the other way around the contestant doesn't care about the crowd either, it's the judges and the winning purses he watches.

Hurst's big success with his "Grand Contest" scattered well throughout the West also some into the East. It was the first two day contest that'd ever been put on or heard of, and with its great success spreading, it wasn't long when many promoters' palms begin to itch. All the information that could be gathered as to the doings in that contest and how it was put on was piled up, and more was added on, with the result that by the time spring come there was rumors of at least a half a dozen contests that was going to be promoted, all by different promoters, some of 'em that would try to promote anything from nothing, and from a flea circus to salting gold mines. It was expected that Randall would sure enough put on another contest and try to imitate Hurst, and sure enough, Nat was notified of it with another folder. It would be a two day contest too, and the prizes would be on the level with the ones Hurst had put up in his latest one.

Well, now, with Randall's contest, which he called "The Cowboy Roundup," and all the other contests that would be put on, by going to the ones where Flint or Mark wouldn't be contesting, Nat figured he'd have more of a chance. Another good thing would be that the best cowboys all around would be more scattered at the different contests, giving him still more chance. Mark thought in about the same way he'd also rather contest where Flint wouldn't be.

As for Flint, he also thought that the more contests the better, the cowboys would scatter more and give many of them more chance at the winnings. He thought too that on that account the Hurst string would be pretty well dodged, for he figured that by now many of the cowboys had found out that there was no tougher and harder bucking horses than them Morte horses was. On that account and with all the other contests going on Hurst would most likely find himself short of contestants so as to put on a good show, and then the only way he'd get 'em would be to raise his prizes. Flint would stick to the Morte string, for they was reliable, not only in doing a top job of bucking, but to carry him to the first prize.

With that combination of Flint's steady winning and the horses' hard bucking reputation there wouldn't be much competition. But Flint wouldn't be sticking only to the Hurst contests, he'd go to others in between times, where the biggest purses would be offered.

Flint rode in eight contests that summer and won first in bucking horse riding at six of 'em. The reason he didn't win at the other two was the same as had been at Randall's contest, and he didn't get no chance to try other horses as he had with Randall, for the judges figured the horses he'd drawed had bucked hard enough, only not hard enough to carry Flint to any of the prizes. That was just his hard luck.

That hard luck didn't worry Flint much this time, he'd got so as to expect such happenings, and his disappointment was eased when Mark was there to win at one of 'em, the only time he'd got to see Mark that summer. That cowboy had done well, he'd come out winner three times out of five contests. He hadn't seen Nat, but heard that he'd done well in steer roping and won one first in bucking horse riding.

"I think Nat is going in for roping more and more all the time." Mark had remarked, "The rough ones are getting the best of him."

Mark had also tried his hand at bull dogging, he'd said, done some practicing on the range and thought he was going pretty good.

When that fall come, Flint had the contesting fever for fair. He'd traveled quite a bit, had considerable fun in meeting up with other cowboys from all parts and seeing different folks and towns, and different countries. It'd got so with him that just riding the rough string while working for some cow outfit or other between contests got to be monotonous. Being at the age he was and with all the encouraging first winnings, he was easy spoiled, and driving or holding a bunch of cattle was only dead necessity, for he had no more interest there. A good cowboy, to stay being one, should never get away from the range.

Flint was a good cowboy and would always be, but for the time his interest for cattle and range had turned to bucking horses, arenas, and prizes. He worked mostly to keep in practice on the rough ones and to keep enough money ahead so he could hit out at the first rumor of a contest coming on. With his work on the range and between contests he'd try to make it with some horse outfit instead of cattle, on account it was faster work, but that couldn't often be managed, for horse outfits was not near as numerous as cow outfits. Another drawback was with the horse outfits shipping out broke and unbroke horses they didn't bother much with horses that was hard to break or turned outlaw, they was just shipped out as unbroke. Flint found his roughest horses with the cow outfits, for with them they wanted to keep every horse that work could be got out of, good or bad. But with some of the horse outfits, Flint found some tough spoiled ones that wasn't shipped, and he *kept* 'em that way. With such outfits he'd get so he couldn't "see" a cow, not even if he ran smack into a bunch of 'em.

The next spring come, and during the early part of it, Hurst put on another contest. It was his first for that year, just to sort of limber his horses up after the long rest and also to add up a little more cash to go on with the contests he had lined up for that year. On account of the now wide reputation of the Morte horses he had the advantage over the other promoters and could get most of the towns he chose.

His first contest for that year was only for one day, but Flint was there, done his usual good riding and again rode off with the first prize. Neither Mark nor Nat had been there, but there'd been others and mighty good riders to compete against.

It was there that Hurst told him he'd spread a couple of his contests to three days that year, and his prizes would be well above what any of the other contests could offer. From the cowboys, Flint also got to hear of quite a few other contests for that year, twice as many as the year before, most of 'em to be two day contests and offering better prizes than before. Only trouble was they was quite a distance apart, and unless a contestant was pretty sure of himself winning fair prizes he wouldn't be making anything in taking 'em on, only the closest ones.

Flint felt he could win at least fair prizes, and now he was going to contest in another event besides bucking horse riding, that was bull dogging. Mark had sort of given him that idea and during the winter past he'd practiced some on that, when the boss wasn't in sight. He'd started on yearlings at first and a few had slipped out from under him, leaving him to land hard but he would get up grinning and try another one, till finally he got to two year olds and then to the full grown, regular bull-dogging steers.

He'd decided to take on other events, too, any and every other kind but roping. Flint hadn't took to roping much, and to be able to catch the horses he wanted, about ended up his ambitions that way. When he did rope a couple of times at contests it was more for the fun of it than with the hope of winning anything, and now, with all the good ropers that came to contest he figured it best for him to forget competing in that event.

So with all the other events he'd decided to enter in and the many contests there'd be that year, Flint didn't figure he'd be doing much range work for some months beginning with July, for, from that month on they would come pretty thick and he'd have to do considerable travelling to be on hand at the contests he'd decided to compete at. Some of 'em would be pretty far East, in thickly settled farming countries acrost the great plains, and he wondered why the prizes of the contests being held there was so much bigger, in such far away land that was no cow country, where there was no cowboys and few of the people had ever heard or knew what a cowboy was. And that was just what raised the prizes, for the cowboys would have a long ways to come to such contests, there'd be more expense. There had to be cowboys and good ones to make the contests good shows, and good prizes is what would bring 'em.

To make up for that and the long distance shipping of the bucking and roping stock it was expected that there'd be much bigger crowds to attend there than in the West.

That was none of Flint's worries, the prizes is what attracted him and he planned on taking in at least two of the two day contests. Hurst wouldn't be going on with his until in the fall and on into the winter. He'd of course put one two day contest on the Fourth and another on Labor Day, and that made it just right for Flint, for in the meantime he could take on some of the other contests he had in mind. As for breaking even on travelling and other expenses, he wasn't worried about that, for he figured that with all the events he'd planned to enter in, he could win enough to at least get back to where he wanted at least in the same comfortable way he'd went, and he'd maybe return packing enough prize money so's to make him stoop-shouldered.

He rode on thru many contests during that summer and even tho the horses didn't give him the chance the Morte breed always did he came on thru with many first prize moneys, and he made fairly well at other new events that was brought on. But even at that he wasn't stooped from packing the prize moneys he'd won, for it took money to travel from one contest to another, and plenty more while waiting at some hotel for the dates, also during the contests. All in all he came thru a lot better than most of the best contestants did, and the one thing that really put the stoop on him was that one day, while all was going well and the contest he'd easily won at in the bucking horse riding was near at an end, a cowboy came to him and informed him of Nat's sudden death. A bucking horse had loosened him, throwed him over forward in front and planted a hard landing hoof on his head, near crushing it into the ground as he bucked on over him. That took plenty of the good feeling from Flint.

Another thing that Flint heard while in his rounds of the contests was that Mark had won first in one bucking horse contest. It had been a big prize, and soon as the entrance fee money was paid, the gate money received, and all other moneys was in at the office, the crooked promoter stuck it all in a bag and hit out for parts unknown.

The contest went on and thru in good shape, none of the cowboys nor anybody else knowing of that promoters hitting out with all the money, and it wasn't until the contest was well over and all of the crowd had gone that it was found out. The trick left many a cowboy stranded and all of 'em mighty sore. That promoter was never seen again by any of the cowboys he'd tricked nor any others who knew him.

Them two happenings took some of the spicing out of contests for Flint and he was kind of glad to get back to a range he knew. It was the ∿, the superintendent was pleased to see him again and the foreman had some more rough ones for him, some of 'em that'd went back to the bad.

That helped some, and then Hurst put on another big two day contest in a town not far away. Flint of course went to it, once more set on the good kinky backs of the Morte horses and then returned to the ∿ again, with the first prize money in his pocket. That outfit was mighty proud of "their" cowboy, Flint.

There was other contests that year, one by Randall, but Flint didn't go. But he did go when Hurst put on two more, over a month apart, and on the second one Hurst came to him grinning and said:

"There's no use of you riding, Flint. You'll get it anyhow, so I'd just as well hand you the money now."

But as freak luck would have it, Flint didn't even make third in the last contest of that year. He'd done fine in the first day's ride, but on the second and for the final decision ride, he drew a head fighter, one of the worst horses in the Morte string. Flint of course knew the horse and had rode him well many times before, but this time, as this head fighter swung his head far to one side and then the other with every crooked jump, then hung it away down and throwed it up again, there was one time when as that horse swung his head away to one side in one jump and then as far down as he could get it in the next, that Flint's hand on the rein was jerked to the saddle horn and then the fork (pommel) during them two wicked jumps.

It was all an accident, and Flint could of let the rein slip thru his hand and rode the horse as well, but the jerks had come so quick and hard that it couldn't be helped. "Touching leather" alone was against the rules and would disqualify a rider, and according to two of the three judges, Flint had not only touched leather but it looked to the judges that he had his closed hand under the horn, near like "pulling leather."

There's no arguing against the judges in their decision in the arena, no more than there is to the judge on the bench in the court room. So Flint just had to grin as later on he remarked to Hurst that he should of took him up when in a joking way, Hurst had said there was no use of his riding and that he'd just as well give him the first prize money then.

It had been a good year for Flint, but when he thought of Nat and Mark and then his own freaky luck the ending hadn't been very good. He was sort of wanting to forget about contests for a while, his fever for them had gone, and he was glad to get back to the ∿ again and compete just by himself against the rough ones there. He was needing a rest.

VIII
A RODEO CROSSES THE OCEAN

FLINT GOT MORE of a rest that winter than he expected. A good January rain and little snow come, lasted two days and then it froze, leaving a good coat of ice over the range, also of course in the corrals where he was more or less steady at the rough ones. In them corrals was deep in the earth granite boulders, some of which stuck up a few inches above it, and their rounded tops was also covered and slick with the icy coat.

Flint set no thoughts to that as he climbed one of the rough ones and unlimbered his quirt along his neck so's to make that ornery pony raise his head, quit his bucking and go to behaving. That horse was at his worst when his front feet glanced on the side of one of the slick boulders as he came down stiff legged. It wasn't just a fall that followed, for with the action that horse was putting on, he hit the slick rock and earth broadside, like to pop and as tho he'd been slammed down from high above. It happened too quick for Flint to get away, and some time afterwards, with his right leg pretty well smashed up from the knee down, made his way to the bunk house. That leg had connected with a couple of the boulders with the heavy horse on top of it as he slid in the hard fall. And the horse, he had a hip crushed in in that fall.

It wasn't just a fall that followed.

It was the hospital and a cast for Flint for over a month, then back to the ∿ camp, still with the cast for another couple of months, then he was supposed to keep off the rough ones even after that and for some time even after the cast was taken off.

Flint had had quite a few accidents before with handling the rough ponies but this was the first one that layed him up for any length of time. He was told by the doctor that it wasn't just a broken leg he had but smashed so that the bones was to splinters, that he was lucky no complications set in and he should be very careful of it for at least a year or he'd have trouble.

But he was there and on the job again when the Fourth of July come and as Hurst put on a big three day contest. He'd been able to wear his boots again for near a month, and bandaging his leg up good and tight as he could before the first day of the contest he again entered in the bucking horse riding event. He done good as ever in the tryout and when it come to the final ride for the decision he done still better, and came to the top as first prize winner once more.

Well, he'd evened things up as to his feelings in being disqualified in the last contest of the year before, even with the breaking of his leg, and he was surprised at himself that he could still do so well after the long layoff he'd had. He felt no bad effects on his bum leg, and it was a good thing he wasn't the kind of rider who rode on his spurs* or he might of felt plenty of bad effects.

He took on near as many contests that year as he did the year before but there was two events which he didn't enter in during that time, that was bull-dogging and the wild horse race. He made out lucky not to hurt his leg, even when some of the bucking horses fell

---

*A rider who clinches or hooks the cinch with his spurs to stay.

with him, and with all the new events that was added on and which he could compete in, he made near as good in winnings as he had the year before. That fall he again came back to the ∿, for two reasons, one to work out the balance of what he owed the outfit for hospital fees and doctor bills they'd paid for him the winter before. He had plenty of money from his winnings to pay that off, but he wanted to keep it, and earn some more to go on contesting with the next year. A feller could never tell what might happen in that game, he found out. The other reason was that they'd have many of the spoiled ones, new and old, for him to take the rough off of, and next to the Morte horses they was the best for him to keep in practice on. They was better than most of the bucking horses that was used in the contests.

As summers and contest seasons and then winters come, Flint managed to get back to the ∿ for some years that followed. His crushed leg, by good luck and health, healed well and one winter, after he'd took in many rodeos, went to bull-dogging again, took on all the events he could and done extra good, he went to visit his home folks. His name as Champion bucking horse rider and all around contestant had spread a considerable by then and he was looked at as quite a hero by all on his home range. His mother, even tho some worried always, was proud of him, and so was his dad who tried to hide his feelings that way by often remarking that this contesting was only for "whistles" (the young and foolish) and wouldn't get a feller nowheres, nothing like settling down to a good bunch of cattle and be sure of a good home and living.

Flint laughed and said he'd come to that some day, when he'd be getting old and decrepit. His younger brother agreed with him and was only sorry that somehow he hadn't turned out to be the rider Flint was. He tried hard enough, he said.

That winter had been pretty idle for Flint, and the next winter after another long summer of contesting he was again at the ∾, with the rough ones there.

Flint went along to contesting year after year, rules changed, new events came on and he fitted himself to 'em so he was such a recognized champion that whenever it came to riding, whether it was bucking horse riding with saddle (it was called saddle bronc riding by then) or bareback or steer or bull riding or any kind of riding, the contesting cowboys throwed up their hands and bid first prize good bye when he come to sight.

He'd come to the Hurst contests whenever he could, to get to sit on the Morte horses again, for he had more affection for 'em than he knew. Them horses had never failed him, there was no "running buckers" amongst any of 'em and they was the foundation of stirring the talent in him and making him the rider he was.

But finally came the time when some of them faithful buckers didn't care to buck no more. They wasn't aggravated to keep on with it. Instead, when they showed sign of quitting, Hurst turned 'em loose on his good range and pensioned 'em. Then he went to try and replace them and then was when he run into great disappointments, for there was no replacing the horses them straight bays had been, or what some of 'em still was.

Flint knew of Hurst's disappointments and done his best to help him, but there was no more such horses, and finally with Hurst's appreciation of Flint, the time come when he asked him to ride the last and only horse left in the Morte string, before that horse would also be pensioned.

There was no quirting nor scratching as that good bucking horse, to the last, was rode, just the motions and like a revered requiem to the Morte string. Flint got first prize for that ride, but to him he thought only of that ride being the last on one of the best and truest bucking horses he'd ever rode.

From then on the contests took Flint to more scattering places, from the Atlantic to the Pacific and from Border to Border. Only a few months in every two years or so would the ∾ see him again, along winters, and then one year at a big Fourth of July contest he got quite a surprise, and a shock. The rules had been made stiffer right along every year in the bucking horse riding, and to where the contestant had to be quite some rider to put up a qualifying ride according to them rules. It got so that the horse had the most advantage.

But it wasn't that that surprised or shocked Flint. It was that with the new and stiffer rules the poorer riders had went to work and remade or deformed their saddles so's they could go by them new rules and still make a ride. They was saddle "made to meet the requirements" as the saddle makers explained, and they was of course glad to oblige and make any kind of saddle that was ordered. So, and the result of such orders, is what made Flint stop and stare in surprise.

He'd come to that big contest to the East, and there, on the railing between the track and the field is where he first got sight of about a dozen of the freaky looking saddles. To him, and many of the other boys gathered around and looking the things over, they didn't look like saddles at first glance, nor even after a closer look. The stirrup leathers, horn and cinch was about all that identified the freaky things as a rig that was made to go on a horse's back.

That epidemic of "freaks" seemed to hit all at once, and many of the cowboys had to laugh and groan at the sight of 'em. The groans was from the mere thought of having to ride a hard bucking horse in one of them contraptions, for if a horse ever got one jump ahead on a rider sitting in such a rig, that rider would sure be whipped to death. It's been said that there's saddles made that can't be bucked out of, but there is no such saddles and if there was nobody but one very ignorant of riding would ever get into it, not even on a gentle trotting horse, let alone a good bucking horse.

That epidemic of freaks that came out that year was the closest to the kind you couldn't get bucked out of that ever was made, and they didn't last long. The riders that got in them was about wedged in by a high and wide fork (pommel) that fitted back into the rider's middle and over the thighs, then the dished in extra high cantle done the rest to do the wedging.

But even at that some of them riders got throwed, some got whipped so their necks about snapped and lost all sense of balance, and the ones that made the first qualifying ride didn't get into the finals and prize moneys, for they wasn't riders or they wouldn't of used such rigs.

There'd been swell forks for years before but they was of medium low swell. Flint had been using one of them on a single three-quarter rigging (one cinch) for a couple of years. The tree was called the Ladesma and covered into the makings of a good comfortable all around stock saddle, but a man had to be a *rider* to stick on a hard bucking horse in one of them, they wasn't "traps" as the freak saddles got to be called.

Flint got to see more such freak saddles at other contests that year. The sight of 'em only put fear in his heart and contempt for the riders that used such contraptions. But he had no fear of competition from them riders, for they was only trying to make up in their saddles for what they lacked in ability, and that didn't work. A few only got hurt because they couldn't get out of their "traps" in time when their horses fell.

Another thing that sent shivers arunning up and down Flint's back that year was the Ladies Bucking Horse Riding event. He'd seen ladies riding bucking horses at contests before, but it'd only be one or two. That had been a sort of interesting surprise, at first, and even tho the girls was good enough riders and the bucking horses was the picked easiest for 'em, Flint soon got so he'd interest himself to looking some other way when he'd hear of one of the fair sex climbing on a bucking horse.

That year there was half a dozen of 'em at one contest. One of 'em got throwed on her head and near broke her neck, and from that time Flint looked the other way more than ever when that event came on.

It was along them years when the cowboy contest promoters got sort of organized, got to know they couldn't do without the range born and raised American cowboy to put on such contests. That of course took in the plains riders of western Canada, also some of the Vaqueros of Mexico. But no imported hands could do, and there's where the American cowboy always has and always will easily hold all championships in that game.

The cowboy contests then got to be called Roundups, Frontier Days, War Bonnet, Fiesta and all different kinds of names, but they was still all contests, and the contesting cowboy today wants it back to that name "Contest," which is sure enough what it is and no show, as far as the cowboy is concerned.

Rodeo, not Rodeeo, which is Spanish for "Round-Up," is nowadays the most used title to cowboy contests. In Mexican language the *e* is mostly pronounced as "ay," and so, Rodeo is pronounced Rodayo, like San Pedro is pronounced San Paydro, and such like.

As the contests got bigger, more numerous and organized there was no such a thing any more as fly-by-night promoters running off with the money gathered in, leaving the cowboys that'd come, contested and won the prizes stranded and a long ways from their home range.

There's no betting at contests, only maybe little private bets amongst friends, so there's no cowboys "bought" to get bucked off, miss in roping or bulldogging so a certain contestant might win. No stock is doped or grogged, and especially with the cowboy, the rodeo is the truest, squarest and hardest fought contest there is. The training is from rough and hard riding from very early ages. There's no scientific managers or sweat shirts or timing in the training, and the cold showers come from the skies while on the home ranges, some times as stinging sleet or snow. But that sort of necessary training as for a living sure wakes up all there is in a man and trains him to be on the lookout far and near for what might come and has to compete against in his profession, such as staying on top a bad horse, heading off or roping renegade stock, to shoving herds towards good shelter during blizzards.

The Rodeos was now beginning to get at full swing, recognized as good attraction, spreading steady and getting more numerous. There was now some four-day contests and with better prizes right along. Then one day there came rumors of a big two-week rodeo that was going to be pulled off away acrost the ocean in Europe. That liked to made Flint and many another cowboy blink and stutter, near knocking the wind out of 'em. There would be powerful big prizes, on account it'd be quite some expense to the cowboy and as only the best was wanted it would take good prizes to draw them.

Flint of course went. He went on the same ship, as did the other contestants, along with the stock, bucking horses, roping and other purpose horses, also long horn steers and all riggings and equipment necessary to put on the big contest.

It was quite some outfit of top cowboys, and good tough stock that wouldn't disappoint neither their riders nor the spectators in what all was expected of 'em. There was a great crowd and grand welcome as the big ship docked at the pier acrost the wide waters, and the way it looked, and all was so well already arranged, it was

135

figured that here would be some record crowd, a chance to the greatest contest as yet and a fine time to be had to boot.

There was no disappointment as to that, crowd, grand stand, arena and all. And with most of the cowboys, seeing how the big grandstand was so filled and all around standing space so crowded, they never thought there was so many people in the world. They'd never seen such a herd of "white faces" all at once. And with the promoter's wise handling and ahead advertising this crowd had got to know and appreciate the fact that this wouldn't be no Wild West show, but a contest amongst the cowboys themselves, like with some of the games in their own land only very strange and much more exciting than any of their own could be.

And there's where the big attraction came in. There was monocled nobility galore in the box seats, and even some royalty at the first day and grand opening of the rodeo, and the tall promoter who knew his cowboys well made quite some impression himself as he rode here and there in the arena, fancy silver mounted rigging and all, on a mighty likely looking horse and to seeing that, with his arena director, every event came on afogging and as it should, no time adragging.

No better, bigger or more appreciating crowd could be asked for on that first day of the grand opening of the rodeo, and to sort of make up for that no cowboy contestants ever turned out any wilder, not with loudness but with action. The only drawback was that the stock, after the many days on the ocean and then being in so different a climate, wasn't quite what they'd been before leaving the American soil. But they still was plenty tough enough, tough enough to make the contesting plenty good, and the cheering crowd was anything but disappointed.

For that contest the cowboys would be getting day moneys, which means that there'd be prizes awarded every day for every event and so as to keep 'em in expense money and "alive," and there would still be the final and big prize on the last day for the ones who'd qualify all the way thru the contest and would be entitled to compete for the grand first prize on the last day. That would be for each event by itself.

But the rodeo didn't get to go on to the grand finals and prizes' day. Crowds came to fill up the grandstand and standing space for a couple more days then the sudden and unexpected come, and it was ordered stopped by the authorities.

It seemed like, as the cowboys got to hear of queer and sudden happenings, that the start of such proceedings was by theatre and different show house owners who by losing many of their patrons which went to the rodeo instead, had got their heads together and finally hatched out a plan to put the kibosh on the rodeo, have it out of the way, and get their patrons back. They couldn't stand a week and a few days more of such a loss, even tho that loss wasn't to such a big percentage, considering.

So they hatched out a plan where, with the willing help of the papers, the rodeo was branded as cruel and inhumane and a disgrace to society. Then the humane officers joined in. It would be great publicity for them as doing a great deed in stopping the rodeo, they might even have their pictures and names in the papers. And so, not seeing the every day suffering horses in their own city, horses that was hooked on to carts or wagons and being jerked thru the streets, shoulders with raw sores, limping from sore feet and half starved most of the time, them officers pounced on the rodeo, and with the authorities backing 'em it was put to a quick stop, regardless whether the crowd in general agreed to it or not, which it didn't.

There was also one happening which had went strong with the humane officers and authorities into deciding against the rodeo and to having it stopped. It was that one of the foreigners had got the fool idea into his head that he could ride one of these "blooming jumping hawses." He'd made quite a beller about it when the arena director tried to tell this loud hombre that it was against the rules to let any outsiders compete, that he had all the contestants he needed, and besides he'd had to enter for the contest the day before it started.

That foreigner couldn't understand all that, and he didn't care to. He kept abellering so, till finally the director not wanting to let him get away with it, consented to let him ride one horse, providing he'd sign an agreement that all responsibilities was on himself, of his own insisting and none on the management, and that was done. This all was afterwards announced to the crowd and explained.

According to this hombre he'd rode in all "sorts" of places, Russia, Australia, Argentine and some more, and like wanting to show the cowboys up he wanted to ride his own saddle. It was a kind of English style saddle but bigger, higher up at the back and with padded like wings which sprouted on each side below the pommel and was used as knee grips.

No special easy or tough horse was picked out for this noisy foreigner, wherever he was from, just one out of the bunch, and the cowboys knew what was going to happen. It happened just as they'd figured only even quicker, and much worse. The foreigner's head went to popping at the first buck. He lost his balance, saddle and all at the third and then, with a good boost the horse sent him aflying high as a kite. When he landed he just crumpled up and layed unconscious. He was still that way when the ambulance whizzed in and took him to the hospital, and he never did regain consciousness. That went well to cap things to stop the rodeo, whose management sure wasn't to blame.

The promoter took quite a big loss at the Rodeo being stopped, a couple or three more days with such good crowds as there'd been and he'd at least broke even. But, as he grinned some time afterwards, he figured himself lucky that with all the oversized talk he wasn't put in jail and have to pay a heavy fine to boot.

As to the cowboys, the ones that won on the daily prizes about broke even, Flint was one of 'em. But the others was only glad to have the chance to return with the stock, and even tho most of 'em was broke and in debt to the ones that'd come out even, it was good to be back on American sod, and as good luck would have it, a good Rodeo, a six day one, was going to be pulled off in a big Eastern town not so far away so's they couldn't make it, at a date that'd give 'em plenty of time to get there to enter, and maybe make enough so they could go on again from there to other contests and make more. This contest had good purses up, and day moneys too.

With that bunch of top contestants, like rescued from a wreckage from acrost the wide waters, which was about true, and now hungry for action, it made some of the contestants already there and entered, wish they hadn't, or wish they'd gone to some other contests. But the promoter, backers and other officials of that contest was mighty pleased, for now, with this unexpected bunch of cowboys which the European country had sent back ahead of time, and the other cowboys already on hand, it'd be a contest where the fur would be sure to fly.

The newspapers made a big thing of the cowboys who'd gone acrost for the contest in the foreign land, what all happened there, how they was glad to get back and so on, and that alone drawed quite an extra and curious crowd, near as interested as the crowds that flocked to see the veterans returning from the World War.

Flint was satisfied in making the finals in that six day rodeo and come out second in the saddle bronc riding. The horse he'd drawed for that ride even tho good wasn't of the best, and he had to make up in riding for what that horse lacked in bucking, in order to make that second prize.

But he made a couple of day moneys in that same event, then again won first in bareback (with surcingle) bronc riding, and one day money in that event also. He made third in bull-dogging, some more in a few other events, and all in all he was pretty well fixed to travel on to some other rodeos. He grinned with the thought, when he come to sum up his winnings, that he even had enough to take him acrost the waters and back again if he wished to, and in good style.

But there was many of the many cowboys gathered there who didn't do near so well, many of 'em didn't win anything at all and slept or rested in the piles of baled hay for the stock, some of 'em badly bruised, cut or with sprained joints, and doing their own bandaging with whatever they could get. Few cowboys ever ride the ambulance away to the hospital when they get hurt, unless they don't know anything about it, when they're unconscious.

A few of these hurt contestants amongst the bales of hay, being broke, was talked into sharing hotel rooms with their own kind, also meals. All was taken care of as is the case amongst cowboys anywheres, that's a bringing up that comes from the range, and when the last day of the rodeo come and all was making ready to hit out for other contests, or home, there was contributions made by most all connected with the rodeo so that none of the stranded and hurt cowboys would be left behind. There was no contributions asked or hinted from any one not connected with the rodeo.

That way only would the cowboy accept any help, for he'd feel that with contesting along at other rodeos later on and coming to the top with better luck, he could return the favor, sometimes to the same ones that had helped, if not to some others who might need help. No real cowboy ever bums, no matter how stranded or in need of help he might be. It's not in his makeup and he'll find a way out.

The next rodeo that Flint took on was further to the west, and he went there for the reason that, after the ocean trip and the last rodeo in the crowded East he was hankering for more open country. He went by automobile to that rodeo, with another contestant by the name of Mike Ryan who went mostly for roping, bulldogging and other events where well reined and good cow horses would be needed. To the back of his car, and for that purpose, was his two top cow horses in a good trailer, going right along with him.

There was quite a few cowboys had got to travel from one contest in their own automobiles by then, some would go in partnership on one, and sometimes there'd be six or eight piled up in one car, with bed rolls, saddles and all, and the wild experiences

141

*There was quite a few cowboys had got to travel from
one contest in their own automobiles by then.*

some of 'em would have in going around the country that way, in
all kinds of roads and weather would make quite some book and
interesting to most automobile drivers, for in many cases them
automobiles was turned pretty well into cow horses.

When Flint and Mike got to their destination they made camp
not far from the grounds where the rodeo was going to be held,
amongst some cottonwoods and by a little stream. There was other
cowboys that'd parked their cars and made camp there, and as Flint
looked around, caught sight of a big car with a sort of covered wagon
trailer attached to it and was squinting at it when he got a surprise,
for by that trailer was a cowboy busy building a fire for the evening,
and that cowboy was none other than Mark.

Flint hadn't seen Mark for some years, and hitting a running walk he was soon by his side and shaking hands with that just as much surprised cowboy. But that wasn't all the surprise, for out of the trailer came a fair looking young lady packing a few dishes and things and setting them on the folding table not far from the fire.

She smiled as she passed Flint, and then he recognized her as a girl he'd seen ride in the ladies' bucking horse contest at a couple of rodeos he'd been to. He'd also seen her in trick riding and she was as good there as in her bucking horse riding, which was very good.

The two had never got acquainted but she'd also recognized Flint, and now, after she'd set the dishes on the table, Mark spoke up and says to him:

"You know Judy Morley, don't you, Flint?"

The girl turned and Flint smiled as he raised his hat. "I've seen her ride a few times," he says to her more than to Mark, "but never got to within speaking distance of the lady."

"Well," Mark grinned at him, "she's not Judy Morley any more. Judy and me was tied in holy wedlock some two years ago, and now meet my wife, Mrs. Mark Hollister."

Mark let that soak in for a spell, and after Flint got over his surprise and congratulated 'em, Mark went on.

"Now we're sure of having bacon and flour in our chuck box," he grinned, "because we never both lose, not even if I see that right now, with you dropping in, I'm out of the first money in bronc riding. But I might make second and besides there's plenty of other events.

"I've been going pretty strong for roping since I seen you last," Mark went on, "and doing good. You know how it is when a cowboy begins to slip in his riding, he goes to roping."

"Yep," says Flint in a joking way, "and gets married."

Flint had to stay for the good supper that Judy and Mark had set up and there was some great visiting talk thru the meal, and afterwards, when Mike joined 'em. Both Mark and Judy already knew Mike, and with the four gathered by the fire there was many contests mentioned where each had been. Many broncs was named and rode, many steers was roped and throwed, and along with Flint's telling of his crossing the sea and his experience with the rodeo in the foreign land, then each taking turns in reminiscing on incidents and accidents with different events, the conversation went on until away late that evening.

Then as Flint and Mike stood up to leave, Mike put in a final remark that he heard there'd be new rules with this contest that was sure tough.

"Let 'em come," Mark grinned, "me and Judy here'll bring home the bacon anyway."

IX

MAKING IT TOUGHER ON THE COWBOY

FLINT, MARK AND MIKE sized up the string of buckers in the big feed corrals the next morning and figured there'd be few if any rerides on them ponies, for every one of 'em sure looked like they was out to get a cowboy down, no just run or crowhopping about them.

Mark grinned a remark that he didn't know wether if to enter in the bucking horse event or not, that he was a married man now and maybe he'd better stick to roping and bull-dogging. As for Mike he didn't care how tough they came out, he'd quit bronc riding anyway. Flint was just as much at ease, for these was just plain broncs to him as compared to the Morte outlaws which he'd never forget.

But there was the rules to be considered, and this man who owned these buckers, his name was Drake, had seen to it that they was made plenty stiff. He was out to build a reputation for his horses so they'd be in demand for the big rodeos and well paying contracts, and them rules was so the horse had about all the advantage and the cowboy near had to be a centipede to go by them rules and make a ride. For the more cowboys was throwed the bigger a reputation his horses would get.

Snubbing in front of the grandstand had long been in the past by then and now, with most big rodeos, there was chutes built where horses was run in from an adjoining corral, and with the broncs in partitions of the chute with a wide gate opening from each, four to ten broncs could be saddled and ready when riders was called to come out on the named and numbered horses.

That style of doing things is not near as interesting to the crowd as the old way of snubbing because they can't very well see the fighting bronc being saddled, but it's faster, and ready bucking horses can come out soon as the one before has done his worst, is picked up and led out acrost the arena to be unsaddled. The steers used for bucking and bull-dogging was handled thru them same chutes, as is done these days, but there's no picking them up and leading them to the corrals acrost the arena, instead most of 'em are ready to hook man or horse on sight, and have to be roped and maneuvered out of the way for the next steer, rider and bull-dogger.

With steer riding, first with rope for a holt, then to surcingle with two hand holts, Drake had changed that rule there and made it a one hand holt rule, where the cowboy was to hold his other hand out or up and not touch the steer with it. He wanted to make a reputation for his steers too.

He also cut out the "hoolahan" in bull-dogging (throwing a steer while on the run) and now a bull-dogger had to stop his steer before he could proceed to try and lay him down. That put Mark out quite a bit, for it took a heavier man to do that and it would be quite a strain on Mark's hundred and fifty pounds.

But that wasn't all. The bronc riding rules was still the toughest and now the cowboy wasn't to ride his own saddle, instead there was introduced a standard saddle, a good enough saddle, but all alike and of the same size excepting maybe in the length of the tree,

He also cut out the "hoolahan" in bull-dogging
(throwing a steer while on the run).

and the slim or stocky cowboys had to fit themselves to them as best they could. Added on to that was a flank rigging, a strap that goes around the horse's flanks and where an ornery bronc is most "ticklish." It acts like and does no more harm than slipping an icicle down somebody's back, or tickling the short ribs.

Another rule was that a rider was no more allowed to quirt or fan with his hat, which both go for quite a bit of balance and help to the rider; then he was to scratch ahead for the first three jumps and back for the next three jumps, all the time the braided bucking rope rein was to be held six inches above the bronc's withers.

Flint was up to ride the first day but only for bareback, so he had that day to study them rules, which if violated meant being disqualified for the event for the rest of the Rodeo. He watched and seen how the riders took to the new stiff rules and seen where not many of 'em had qualified for the semi-finals. That was another thing that was brought on that was new to many a cowboy, the semi-finals, where the rider who qualified from the tryout would have to ride again to make the finals, and again at the finals and for the prize. Many riders are eliminated by that time, some of 'em as good as the best, but the bronc and part he plays in that game has a considerable to do as to how far a rider can get.

It was a surprise and puzzle to Flint that first day when, as the broncs was being lined into the saddling chutes, he seen Drake going along it and reaching thru the gate timbers chalking a line along the side of each horse's withers which marked the limit as to how far ahead the saddle was to be set. The more ahead and on the withers a saddle is set the less back jolts and twists a rider gets, and to make the riding of his broncs all the harder he seen to it that the saddles was set fair middle and not over his chalk mark.

That made Flint grin to himself, for he'd learned to ride rough ones in the old slick-fork double rigs, and them rigs set well back to where every jolt and twist can't be missed. He'd rode the Morte horses that way and now he noticed that even tho the chalk mark was well back, it wasn't any further back than where his old double-riggin used to sit. He also noticed that these new all-alike saddles wasn't as low and narrow forked or as slick as the one he'd been riding; there was more to grip to in them than with his, and even tho Flint didn't ride on grip he seen where they might be of some advantage.

The Rodeo Association which was formed about then was responsible for bringing out the standard rodeo saddle, eliminating the freak ones that had been used by some of the poorer riders. The saddle was and is called The Association and is used at every rodeo belonging to the A.R.A., an association where no championship or points are recognized unless the contestant contests at a rodeo belonging to it.

On account this perticular rodeo was with the association and many rules was new, Flint was sort of glad that he wasn't up for anything but bareback bronc riding that first day. He done his usual very good, and the rest of the time he had, gave him a chance to watch and sort of get next to the goings on.

Mark came out on saddle-bronc-riding and was surprised to learn that night that he'd qualified for the semi-finals.

"Doggone it," he says, all pleased, "them Association rigs ain't bad at all."

Mike also had a chance to use his two good horses on the two events he'd entered in, single steer roping and bull-dogging. He made well above average on time for that day.

So, all in all, the three cowboys and Judy was well pleased, and now, for the next day, Flint drawed a horse by the name of Stargazer, the most peaceful and quiet sounding name that Drake had attached to any of his buckers, for with the others there was such scary names as Hell-Bent, Thunderbolt, Fit-to-Kill, Tombstone and such like.

But Flint wasn't to be fooled by the quiet name of Stargazer, for he might turn out to be a star hazer instead.

And he come near being just that when Flint came out of the chute on him the next day. That bronc turned on most of the tricks of a top bucking horse, near as good as the Morte horses.

There was one time when that bronc put his head down so far that he jerked Flint's hand to the withers for a couple of jumps. Then again, instead of the new saddle being of some advantage, as he'd thought, it was only a sort of a handicap in not being used to it. But as the judges watched him thru the first few hard jumps, the way he rode, free and easy, they already had him down for the semi-finals. It was an even up best ride of the day.

Mark came out on the horns of a big steer in bulldogging, the biggest steer there was in the bunch and tossed that cowboy over the track railing. "No time."

But Judy, his wife, done well in the cowgirls' bronc riding and made a good start for the money. Then with her trick riding which is paid by contract, like with trick roping and all such which is exhibition and no contest, there was, as Mark had said, some more added to the larder for them two that day, even if one had lost.

Mike along with the renting of his horses for roping and bull-dogging made enough to more than double pay for feed and all expenses. A good horse for them two events goes a long ways towards bringing a cowboy to the winnings.

As Drake had it well advertised, and with the help of the stiff rules, his broncs and wild longhorns made a fine showing. The advantage being most all on them there was quite a few cowboys throwed, which pleased Drake, for that gave his stock all the more notorious reputation for rodeo purposes.

The crowd too thrilled more, still does, and always will, at seeing a cowboy being throwed and stomped on than to see him make a good straight up ride. The sympathy is for the animals, thinking they're being abused and made to be mean. It's all to the contrary, for a horse that has to be made to buck never makes a good one, and so, never makes a good showing. Besides there's so many natural born outlaws that's inclined to do nothing else but fight and buck, there'd be no sense in trying to make a bad horse out of one that's well behaving.

The bucking horse at the rodeos is the most well taken care of, and as for the steers bucking and fighting it's them longhorns' instinct. If a feller was to wait, as the old saying goes, "till the cows come home" he'd be a Rip Van Winkle and still have to wait and them cattle would be out in the rough hills they come out of, hard to see and reach and wild as antelope.

There was many other events at that rodeo, such as the Roman Race where a cowboy stands up on two horses with one foot on each race horse. With three or four teams racing around the track that way and crowding the rail, a pony's bare back can get pretty slippery. There was the Chariot Races, with three or four horses hooked abreast, all decorated up as Nero most likely had 'em, a little old gold flowered chariot abobbing up behind the racing team and a cowboy riding it. Them was pretty but mighty reckless races. At one time two of the racing teams got tangled up, horses mixed and piled up and one chariot, with the cowboy driver still in it, was stood straight up on the end of the tongue and throwed plum over the mixed up teams, cowboy and all.

There was stage coach races with just as bad mixups and many other kinds of races, the funniest one being the pack race, where the cowboys stand in line on their saddle horses, and pack horses with regular cowboy bedding squaw-hitched onto 'em.

At a shot the whole outfit started, went full speed to a line where the bed horses was unpacked, the bed spread out on the ground and each cowboy crawling into them like for the night. But only the motions was gone thru. Each cowboy had to lay flat in his bed, and that was all that was necessary, then they jumped out, squaw-hitched their beds on their pack horses again, got on their saddle horses and raced back to the starting point. The first man there of course won, but not before the hitch and the way the bed was packed was examined and tied as it should.

Amongst the many events there was also bull fighting but not of the kind as is done in Spain or Mexico. There was no banderillos (barbed prods) stuck in the bull's shoulder to make him mad, some of them bulls didn't need any. The bull fighters was from Mexico and didn't use no Muleta (cloak) nor anything to leading the fighting bull in missing his man, the man was just supposed to dodge at the right time, and sometimes he didn't. When he didn't he'd be tossed ten feet or more in the air, the bull would catch him coming down and toss him up again, and when things got too rough cowboys rode up to attract the bull from his victim. Them bull fighters had to quit after the second day.

Even the clown would go to bull fighting, but in his own way. He'd stand up in a barrel and when the bull would come too close he'd duck down in the barrel, then jump up again like a jack in the box as the bull looked around sort of puzzled, but on the third day one bull took that barrel, clown and all for a roll and kept a hooking and rolling it till it fell apart. As good luck would have it the clown was close to the tall Arena fence and he made it in time. When the bull turned to go on, the clown jumped down and started after him, until that bull turned again.

Between bucking stock events, and while such stock was being handled from one corral to another and made ready in the chutes there was more races, such as the relay race which idea originates from the Pony Express and where horses are stationed and held ready for when the racing rider rides in, slides off his horse while he's still on the run, pulls the saddle off of him and slaps it on a fresh horse which starts at full speed from a standstill, the rider hanging on to his side for a short ways. His boot heels hit the ground once and he lands up in the saddle while the horse is at a dead run. It sometimes takes less than five seconds to unsaddle and saddle, change from one horse to another and be gone again. There was four changes in that relay race.

The relay race, which idea originates from the Pony Express.

There was also sulky races, but the race that beat them all and always will, for action, was the wild horse race which wound up each day's contest.

The third day and time for semi-finals come. By helping with handling the stock and riding an association saddle the while, Flint kind of got used to the new rigging, and when come his time to ride he done that in grand style on a good hard horse that easy qualified him for the finals.

Mark rode well and on a good horse too but he didn't quite make it, there was too many already up for the finals anyway. But he made it in bareback bronc riding, and even tho he was out in bull-dogging he was fourth in steer roping. Mike was third, in both roping and bull-dogging.

Flint had got well onto the hang of association rig when the fourth day and his time to ride come, and when the grand finals was over, the dust settled and the sun set at the cowboys' camps amongst the cottonwoods that evening, he had a five hundred dollar check in his pocket for first prize in saddle bronc riding, also, by Mike's car, a fancy saddle, presented to him by the commercial and other clubs of that town. The saddle, as it is with most prize saddles, wasn't to his taste, he would take it and his old slick one at some saddle shop to be sold and he'd get himself a plain one on an association tree, for he figured he'd better get well used to that rig for the future contests.

Mark and Judy about broke even in their winnings, with Mark a little in the lead. He'd won second in bareback bronc riding and third in steer roping. Judy had also won second in Cowgirls' bronc riding and then there was her pay for trick riding.

Second prize was won by Mike too, in both steer roping and bull-dogging, and then a fair amount was made thru the renting of his horses to other contestants.

So, all in all, and considering the many good hands they had to compete against, the four felt they'd done mighty well, but not any better than they deserved, for them four sure wasn't at all easy to hold a candle to.

Mike drove to town that evening, taking his two-horse trailer and brought back a bale of good hay and some grain for his ponies.

Flint went along with him and brought back some good red beef and other victuals for all four, also some bottled up cordiality to sort of celebrate, for on the next day they'd all be going different ways, all of course but Mark and Judy who'd be riding shoulder to shoulder, but in some other direction than either Flint or Mike would be taking, and it might be months, or even years before they'd all get together again. Many things could happen in that time, specially in that game of contesting.

Being there was a month or more before there'd be any contests worth while traveling to, Flint decided to hit back for the edge of the desert and the old ∾ outfit. They'd most likely have another of the same bunch of rough ones for him to stomp onto. He felt like he needed a rest from crowds and arenas, and he was some homesick for that range too.

Mark and Judy hinted strong of some "paradise of a little country" along the breaks of a river they knew away to the West where they might build themselves a home and raise a few cattle and some good horses. And some chickens, Judy added on.

As for Mike it was a toss up with him, anyway the wind blew as long as it blew to the West, where he could find a job on a good cow outfit so he could keep up practice on his roping and where his ponies would get good rest and feed.

So, as it was, early the next morning, one car with a canvas covered trailer started out one way, another with a two-horse trailer and two good horses in it went another. And in the town, sometime later, a train pulled out, a cowboy was in the smoker, in the baggage car was his prize saddle and an old slick one, all headed for the home ranges.

X

IT'S ALL IN THE GAME

I T WAS MUCH more than a month or two later before Flint decided there was any contests worth while traveling to. It was
near a year, and in all that time he kept to the rough ones of
the 〜, not so much in the corrals at the main camp no more, but
out on the range and doing regular cow work with 'em, even to
such as roping and cutting out. He was getting good pay for that
work and besides he was relieved of having to stand dayherd, and
night guard, which is a work no cowboy cares much for. Not enough
action.

But to make up for that he took the rough out of more ornery
outlaws than any cowboy that outfit could remember having. He
went thru string after string of them rough ones, and this time,
after he got thru with 'em and each string was turned over to the
other riders, they most of 'em stayed fairly good and so work could
be done with 'em.

His staying with the outfit and not contesting for so long was for
more than one reason. He wanted to limber up on his roping and
try to win a prize at that, and he was given all the chances he wanted,
for there's nothing like good heavy roping to jerk the meanness out
of a bad horse and make him pay attention to cow work instead of
watching for chances to buck his man off.

157

He wanted to limber up his roping.

It was getting late summer when he heard there would be a couple of good rodeos away to the East that offered good prizes, and it seemed like more and more of 'em was being pulled off in many new places and from coast to coast. Flint came near going to the two big eastern contests but by the time he'd make up his mind to go, each one would be about to start and he'd been too late by the time he got there.

In the meantime, Flint didn't get stale in his hibernating from following the contests, not with the work he was doing. Instead, he'd developed a good rope arm and aim and he figured he'd have a chance in the roping event which put up near as big a purse for that as for saddle-bronc riding, and his bronc riding was of course as good as ever. He'd long ago got rid of his prize saddle and the old slick one and been riding the association rig ever since his return to the ⌒. He got well used to it, and now he figured he could put up a lot better ride in it than he had at the last rodeo where he'd contested near a year before in the same kind of rig, and where he'd won first.

With the reputation Flint had made for himself and before the following year's rodeo season really opened, he begin to receive notice after notice from different rodeos that was to be pulled off here and there and everywhere, seemed like. They was more numerous than ever before and all wanted him. For a famous contestant such as Flint had got to be was a good attraction and help to bring in the crowds. Most of the crowds had got to know their cowboys by then, and that if such as him would be there it was bound to be good or he wouldn't come.

It's a great help with any rodeo management to make publicity of the names of the top contestants who will be on hand to compete, along with a recognized string of good buckers. It gets around and is paid attention to in its class near as much as with big games, and the rodeo, once understood by the public, will some day be as popular as any of 'em.

Along with the notices and invitations to come and compete there was prize lists and rules, events and all listed, and with some of the rodeo rules, specially the ones from the East, it was requested that every contestant ride in the parades, something a cowboy always tries to dodge, too much show off. And besides it was requested they all wear loud colored silk shirts, bandanas and other wild west trimmings to conform with the idea the East had of the cowboy. It was mentioned on the rules slips that any contestant failing in that request would not be allowed to compete in the rodeo.

That made Flint grin and snicker. He'd never wore any loud stuff in his life. But he noticed that some of them contests requesting the contestants to parade and play wild west paid the biggest prizes, well worth traveling the long distances to them, and after considering, he thought it might also be worth swallowing his pride for and getting loud, as they wished.

He was glad when one day he received a letter from Hurst, Hurst of the Morte string. There was no mention of parade riding or loud shirts being necessary there, and even tho the prizes wasn't big it was a three-day contest, not so far away and would be a sort of a primer for the following contests.

But Flint didn't need no priming. Hurst put on a good contest and all around show. His string of bucking horses averaged above many of other contests, and besides Hurst had a good bunch of long-legged longhorned brahma steers for the steer riding event. Them steers was half-breed brahman (India cattle) and the Mexico longhorn, and that mixture was fast getting a reputation of being about the hardest thing to ride there was, much harder than the straight longhorn or any other breed. The cross with the longhorn, and running free on the southern ranges, took everything sacred out of them India cattle and put the devil there instead. They was imported and crossed on account they don't get the tick fever or blackleg which puts down many of the other breed of cattle. Now the tall and wiry steers of that breed are used for the steer riding event at all good contests and never fail to do a good job of twisty crooked bucking and fighting, replacing the straight "Sonora Red" longhorn which is now used only for roping and bull-dogging.

Flint didn't enter in that event of brahma steer riding, for he figured he'd entered in enough other events to do him, which was saddle and bareback bronc riding, steer roping and bull-dogging, and just for the fun of it he also entered in the wild horse race.

But as it was with his early raising and from there on, the saddle had been and was still his best bet, and when the contest was over he as usual won first in saddle bronc riding, but no money in bareback, only close for third in steer roping and bull-dogging but not quite close enough, and as for the wild horse race he couldn't scare his horse to line out to race, that pony just stood in one spot, spinned and bucked. Well, that was only for fun anyway.

There was a few weeks before the next rodeo. It was quite a ways to the north. It was a big one and he'd have to buy some loud shirts and such stuff to ride in the parade and to compete in that one, but the prizes was good and he decided to take it in. He headed that direction, and a little over halfways there he run into a cowman on the train who wanted a few colts broke. Them colts was from three to five year olds and that work struck Flint just right to use up the few weeks' time in a good way before the rodeo came off.

He took care of the colts in good shape and even tho none was rough enough to give him good practice, they kept him limbered up, it was much better than laying around doing nothing. He turned 'em over to the old cowman, remarking that he wasn't no hand at teaching a horse anything much, he could only ride 'em. But the old cowman was well satisfied, saying that his cowboys could do the teaching while working 'em with the herds.

Flint got his pay for the job, eight dollars a head, ten head, eighty dollars added on to many times more which he already had, and no time wasted.

He got to the town where the rodeo was to be pulled off, a couple of days ahead of time, and he was surprised to see the many cowboys already there, quite a few of the old hands that he knew and contested with at many other rodeos, far and wide. There was even a few of the top ones he'd went acrost the waters with. There was also quite a sprinkling of the younger cowboys, wiry as steel cables and could take a bronc's hard kick plum center without flinching. Flint didn't know many of these, for most of 'em hadn't been contesting long and hadn't as yet scattered much, but they most all knew or had heard of him, and he seen that all around and with the older top hands he'd have to pull his hat down tight, pull up his shap belt and *ride* if he was going to be in the money in any of the events.

While moseying around, Flint kept an eye peeled for Mark and Judy, and Mike with his two horses but there was no sign of their camps nowheres. Then he got to thinking, maybe Mark and Judy was building up on the little place they'd hinted about the year before. As for Mike there was no telling where he might be. He inquired about 'em a little amongst the older hands but none had seen any of 'em yet that year.

Quite a few of the cowboys was broke and got there in any way they could, all excepting by thumbing their way or riding the rods. The ones that rode the freights came with shipments of stock or paid what they could for the privilege, others piled into automobiles owned by other cowboys, and some rode in from long distances on horseback. Them empty pocket boys was there to win or bust. They'd be hard to contest against, but not many of them had any or enough money to pay their entrance fees for the events they'd come to contest in.

Flint and some of the other cowboys that was better off paid the entrance fees for quite a few of the hard up brethren, even tho these would be entered in some of the same events and contesting against the ones him and others were entering in.

The stable and feed-yard men was also hit by hard up gentry, and some of them being good hands only down in their luck for the time got entered, sometimes with promises of half the winnings in return for the backing. Not many such backers would lose out because they most always knew their cowboys, and if them boys didn't win at that contest they'd most likely make it up at another.

It was Flint's first time at that rodeo and he was glad he came, for it looked like it'd be a good one. Contesting cowboys kept adrifting in from all directions up to the morning of the opening day. A great parade was put on that morning, made up of a good loud band and rodeo officials and the town's mayor in the lead, followed up by a double string of world's champion cowboys and cowgirls and judges, trick riders and ropers, then a mighty colorful two hundred full feathered and war-painted Indians of that state, with women and papooses brought up the rear. Trailing after them was the usual bunch of non-contestants which by riding in the parade would be given a ticket to get in the bleachers, but not in the arena, and their horses was left tied outside of the grounds.

Flint not wanting to pretty up any louder than he could help got himself a dark blue silk shirt and topped it off with a red silk neckerchief, just so he'd pass. He passed, but he sure didn't make no showing as compared to some of the officials and the mayor. The whole townspeople had also sure gone colorful and "Western," as they called it, so did the thousands of newcomers from neighboring and further away states. Most everybody, from small kids to thick-waisted, well-aged business men had went and decorated themselves with the loudest, all color of the rainbow, shirts and neckerchiefs they could get, also the biggest hats and fanciest "hand-me-down" (ready made) boots.

With such a crowd, averaging thirty deep, lining both sides of the streets and with all the bright colors ashining to the sun all around, Flint had to blink. He'd seen some colorful doings before but this one shadowed all of 'em. There was flags and banners everywhere and along with the band aplaying, there was whoops and hollers, as much from the crowds lining the streets as there was from the riders. The cowboys was asked to holler and act as wild as they wanted so long as they didn't get too far out of line and break up the parade. But the spirit of the occasion was in the air and every once in a while some half-broke bronc fresh from the hills would get spooked at all the noise and people, go to bucking and maybe start a few others to do the same, scattering the crowds in good shape.

The parades was put on every morning of the whole six days of the rodeo, and from along about middle forenoon, when the fun started during the afternoon contests, and in the eating and drinking places afterwards and then the Western dance halls, it lasted until away past the middle of the night, sometimes daybreak. The townfolks and visitors all turned wild and wooly during that time, like on a big celebration which it really was, and most everything went.

Flint rode like a wolf during the contest and made the grand finals. He was setting away high in points and up for the first, but his luck failed him at the last. The first final horse he drew was so all het up in his bucking that he forgot about his landing. He went high in the air in about the third jump, twisted up there, and when he came down he turned and rolled plumb over Flint. The cowboy's good angel must of been with him, for he got up on his feet most as quick as the horse did, without a blemish.

He of course got a reride but that second final horse, even tho plenty rough, wasn't the best, just good enough to carry him to second prize, which was plenty fine for all the competition there was at that rodeo. The first horse would of carried him to first, if that horse had stood up.

That made him sort of peeved, so, when it come to his last time in bull-dogging he took it out on the steer. He near hoolihaned him instead of stopping him before throwing, but it wasn't enough so the judges paid any attention, and his peeved feeling turned to pleased surprise when he learned at the rodeo headquarters that evening that his time added as the best and he was officially declared champion bull-dogger right there. That rodeo had the authority to grant that title. His time had been checked up with all record times of the Rodeo Association, and even tho it was just by a few seconds, Flint had made it, and besides the prize money he received the next day he was handed a two hundred dollar gold and silver buckled belt with big engraving as to what it was for and his name also engraved in the center of it, proving that he had.

Of all the championships Flint ever expected of winning, bull-dogging was about the last. Like with his roping he would never expect to get over third there, if he got that. Saddle bronc riding was the championship he'd aimed for and expected most to get. He was rating mighty high already and now feeling sort of conscious of the one championship belt at his waist, he was going to ride for another, with the words saddle bronc riding engraved on it.

He rode harder than ever before that year, took on every big contest he could get to and rode rough ones in between rodeos. He made six first moneys at big rodeos during that time, another first and two seconds at bull-dogging and averaged close time for third at roping, but never close enough. He'd done better time on the range, even on the spoiled outlaws that knew nothing about a rope excepting to have one around their neck when caught or around their ankles when saddled. Roping on the range and in an arena is very different. A cowboy might be good out there in the hills and feel sure of his aim, and turn around and miss his two throws in an arena, and what partly causes the difference is there's a prize to rope for in an arena and many ropers get too tense and careful, where on the range it's only in the day's work and the cowboy doesn't lose anything if he misses there once in a while. Consequence is, he seldom does.

But Flint wasn't so worried about his roping right then. He still held his championship in bull-dogging, and now he was after the one in saddle bronc riding, the highest honor in the contest game.

He got his chance, and after that summer's contesting at many rodeos he was in fine trim to take on a best one. It was a best one, a nine-day one that would be pulled off late that fall, and from the rodeo he'd next be going to he'd have only two weeks to wait till time for the big nine-day one. It would be held in a big city to the east, the prizes was big and a championship would be recognized there too.

As usual he made it to the spot of the doings a couple of days ahead of time, went to the rodeo headquarters and entered in bronc riding, bull-dogging and steer roping. He left out the bareback bronc riding this time, then he went to take a look at the stock. The stock, feed and all was under the wide and long stretch of the grandstand seats. There was the neat, trim and well groomed ponies belonging to the trick ropers and riders wallowing in good feed and bedding, all tied up in a long line which run into another long line of fancy parade horses which was also kept mighty well groomed.

But in a couple of big pens, and loose, there was more horses and these wasn't groomed. An old saying goes for anything wild such as "Never was curried below the knees" but with these they'd never been curried no place, a good free roll in the dirt was better to them than any currying, and as Flint came near he was greeted by some good loud snorts. These was the tough bucking horses, in one pen, and in the other was the just plain wild horses, for bareback bronc riding and wild horse races. All the horses was in fine shape to make a cowboy ride and wallowing in as much and good feed as the groomed ones was.

In two other pens was the cattle. Tall, hump-wethered Brahma steers raised their heads high and shook their long horns at Flint as he went by. Throwing his coat over the high fence and amongst 'em would of been a good way to have it ripped to shreds in short time.

The "Sonora Reds" or Mexican longhorns in the big feeding pen adjoining wasn't so ready to want to fight, not without some cause. If they could run that's all they wanted, and wouldn't turn on a rider unless kept from going where they wanted to. That's why they was so good for roping and bull-dogging, for they'd most always make a bee line from the chutes to the other end of the arena where they'd be turned in the feed pen again and away from the crowds, which they'd never get used to.

Flint seen they was in fine shape for fast roping but would be kind of tough for bull-dogging because they was plenty big and anything but weary looking.

He moseyed around, stopped now and again to visit with the many cowboys he knew and contested with. They was scattered everywheres, amongst the line of horses, many of which was bull-dogging and roping horses owned and brought in by the contestants. Trick ropers was unlimbering their ropes, and here and there amongst the bales of hay was more contestants confabbing in groups and generally taking it easy. The most of 'em had come a long ways, some in many different ways and detours that wasn't smooth, and was now resting.

It was as Flint was moseying around that way that he wound back to the line of the well groomed horses of the trick riders and ropers, and happening to glance between two of 'em as he was going along, he spotted a lone and sort of dejected looking figure at the horses' head, squatted in the hay against the wall, knees up and arms and head resting on 'em. It was a girl.

Flint stopped and took a long squint at her. He couldn't see her face but her general appearance looked sort of familiar, the shirt and the riding skirt. Then looking at her boot tops and the design on 'em it came to him mighty quick as to who the girl was. The design on the boot tops had been of her own idea and order. Amongst the many rows of flower design stitching and in front center of the tops, was a small inlaid piece of white leather in the shape of a horse rearing straight up and without rider. They was very neat and pretty boot tops, for a girl, and even tho it'd been near two years since he'd seen 'em he was quick in recognizing 'em.

But as he walked in between the horses and called the girl by name, he was near stumped for a spell as she raised her head and looked up at him. If she hadn't showed surprise and signs that she recognized him he would of apologized and backed out, thinking he'd made a mistake, for the face sure didn't look much like the same that belonged to them boots with the white horse inlay. It was drawn thin, haggard and there was dark circles around the eyes.

She run the palm of her hand acrost her forehead, smiled a little, and then in a sort of far away voice she said: "I just got in a little while ago with my Poco here," she motioned towards the mighty pretty chestnut horse near her, "I came over two thousand miles and I'm awful tired."

Flint didn't want to ask right then but it slipped out regardless "Where's Mark?"

He spotted a lone and sort of dejected looking figure at the horse's head.

"He's West, home with an old neighbor sourdough who is taking care of him."

That was plenty enough said for Flint. Mark had got busted up and so he couldn't come. While he digested that there was other things he noticed about the girl which showed plain of her circumstances and what all she'd been thru. Her once pretty boots was peeled at the toes and wore thin other places, her once also pretty riding skirt had lost many fringes and silver ornaments at belt and pockets, and her silk shirt showed some patches. Her hat sure needed cleaning and blocking too. Then he noticed her once admired saddle hanging up by one stirrup in front of her horse. It showed plenty of wear, so did the bridle and rest of the outfit.

"Bring your cases here, Judy?" Flint asked, "or are they still in your car?"

She stood up, and pointed down at one case, she'd been sitting on it. "This is all I brought," she says. "We have no more car nor trailer."

Flint didn't stop to ask any questions there, he just picked up the suit case, took a hold of her arm and says, "Come on, Judy, you're going to a good hotel, fill up, clean up and rest up."

There was no balking nor questioning look as she went along, she knew Flint's breed of cowboys.

On the way out, Flint told some of the contestants he knew and which would be around most of the time, some of 'em to even bed down there for the night, to keep an eye on the chestnut and the rigging ahanging in front of him. They sure would, they said. Some of them knew Judy but none recognized her right then.

There was plenty of waiting taxicabs just outside the gate of the rodeo grounds, and helping Judy into one of 'em the two was soon to a good hotel close to the grounds and where quite a few of the cowboys stopped, them that could afford the rates there.

Up in the big sunny room and while Judy was washing and fixing her hair, Flint had a bellhop bring a menu card, and not bothering to ask what she might want to eat he went to ordering. As he hadn't et for quite a while himself he ordered for two, and to have it rushed.

Flint was smoking and looking out the window when Judy came back into the room, looking some refreshed and a little like herself.

"Ain't hungry, are you?" asks Flint.

There was a knock at the door about the same time Flint spoke. He opened it and a good sized tray table was wheeled in, all loaded with the sort of victuals that'd make a feller eat more even if he was foundered. Judy's eyes brightened up at the sight and then she looked at Flint who, expecting such, was looking down at the table while the waiter was arranging things, and smiling, like he was thinking of nothing else but what he was looking at.

The talk was pretty well one-sided during the meal, Flint doing most all of it, about himself, where all he'd been and how he'd done that summer. It wasn't like Flint to talk about himself so much but he wanted to make it so that no talk of Mark or what she'd been thru would be brought up. Besides, his rambling on made her more at ease to eat to her heart's content, and she was sure doing well.

He'd at first thought of ordering only for one and leave her to eat alone, but he'd thought again, like for himself, he'd sure welcome the company of a friend if he hit a big town, broke, all in, and hungry. So, figuring that way, he'd stayed.

Judy was still doing well when Flint quit and stood up. "Don't mind me, Judy," he says. "I had a big feed only a couple of hours ago," he lied, "and what I crave most right now is a smoke."

He walked to the window, rolled a smoke, and looking down the wide busy street, he kept on talking.

"They sure must have a lot of electricity to waste around here," he once remarked, just to make talk. "It's still daylight and they've got all the street lights on already. But," he added on, "it's pretty high here and more light than it is down in that canyon."

Judy et on in peace until finally she pushed back her chair, saying that she figured she'd sure done the good meal justice, and ought to be ashamed of herself for eating as much as she had.

"It's fine to have an appetite," Flint says, "because there's real enjoyment to a meal then."

"Yes," Judy replies, mighty frank, "if you have the meal."

Flint didn't let on like he heard that last. He rolled the table out in the hall so she wouldn't be bothered by the waiter coming up to get it, then getting his hat he made ready to go, saying he'd be staying in the same hotel and would call up her room later if she wished, that she'd better take a nap now and he would go back to the grounds and see to her horse and outfit. There was no comment as to that from her, only a grateful smile.

He was about to open the door when he turned to ask. "How about your contract for the trick riding, have you got that settled?"

"Yes," says Judy; "that was done before I left the ranch. If it hadn't been for that I couldn't have come."

"And about bronc riding," Flint went on; "you're not going to enter in that event, are you?"

"Why, yes, I thought I would. Why?"

"Well, we'll talk that over in the morning. Plenty of time to enter tomorrow anyway. Better get comfortable and rest up now."

"All right, but I would like to see you this evening sometime. I want to talk to you about, about Mark."

The rodeo grounds was dark when Flint got there and when he come to the well lighted feeding pens most of the cowboys had gone, to eat and scatter for the night. He watered and fed Judy's horse some grain, seen to it he had plenty of hay, and after talking to the cowboys around for quite a spell, he hit back for the hotel, got himself a room and taking off only his coat and small hat which he used only on the streets, he stretched out full length on top of the bed. He was a little tired too.

He went to sleep, and he was sleeping sound when along about nine that evening his phone rang. It was Judy calling and wanting him to come see her. She had had a good rest and would like to talk to him a bit before she went to bed for the night.

Flint splashed water on his face and was up to her room in a short while. He was surprised when he seen her that she looked quite a bit like the Judy of a couple of years ago again.

The talk was about the contest for a spell, who all had showed up, prizes and what might be expected, then the subject that was most in Judy's mind came up. It was about Mark, and Judy knowing how him and Flint was such good friends, had rode for the same outfits and contested together for so long, she felt free and relieved to be able to talk to Flint about him.

"He sure thinks a lot of you," she said once. "It seems like, to him, there's only one cowboy, and that's you.

Flint squirmed, and grinned. "Well, he sure ain't no slouch himself," he said.

As Judy went on to tell what had happened, it seemed as tho Mark had beat Old Man Time by only the length of his spur shanks. With the narrow escapes, he had a heap of tough luck, and all at once. The start of it was when he lit on a steer in bull-dogging and something went wrong, such as often happens in any rodeo event. Anyway the steer fell as Mark lit on him, which is something that seldom happens, but it did, and as the steer fell, his head under him, he rammed a horn right thru the inside of Mark's leg halfways up above the knee and that horn sure didn't do no good to the ligaments there.

Lucky the steer turned over so the horn slipped out, for if he'd got up with that holt aholding, he could of done Mark considerable more damage. As it was, Mark raised up out of the dust as the steer went on and walked to the waiting ambulances without anybody hardly knowing of his hurt. At one of the ambulances the blood flow was checked. It was quite some wound but it was treated well right there and bandaged, and regardless of advice and orders that he should be taken to the hospital, Mark had walked out on 'em, remarking that he had to ride in the semi-finals that afternoon

"Damn fools, these cowboys," said one of the ambulance doctors.

Mark, his leg hurting and getting mighty stiff, did come out on the horse he drawed for that afternoon, and on that crazy, head-fighting, crooked and hard-hitting horse he forgot the pain and stiffness in his leg. He couldn't afford to think of that right then, and even done some scratching with that hurt leg of his.

"He'd made the ride and maybe qualified for the finals," Judy said, "but at about the eighth jump the horse near fell. Mark loosened from him, then the horse got his footing again and went at it harder than ever. The horse got up so quick that Mark never did get to sit right in the saddle again, and after a few more jumps that horse upended and he didn't fall, he just throwed himself and popped, right on top of Mark. I could hear things crack even from the chutes, and when the horse got up again and bucked away with the empty saddle, Mark layed where he was, unconscious.

"The ambulance took him to the hospital that time, without his knowing anything about it. He didn't know anything for quite a while after he was wheeled in there, and it was found he had a badly crushed hip, on the same side his leg had been gored thru just a few hours before." The boys afterwards showed Judy the saddle Mark had been riding when the horse throwed himself. The horse had landed so hard that the cantle was mashed flat and layed back. That cantle is what had done the damage.

"It will be a year ago a few days from now when that happened, and in this very same arena we'll be riding in about that time, right here."

There hadn't been much hope for the cowboy for a while, but he made it, layed in the hospital for some months, and then was shipped and carted home in a wheel chair he wasn't to get out of for some more long months. He could walk a little when she left, Judy said, but his hurt hip had shortened his leg a couple of inches and she doubted if he could ever ride much again, sure not bucking horses anyway.

To meet up with hospital and doctor bills all the cattle which they'd bought with their savings had to be sold, also the car and trailer, even down to Judy's chickens, and now all they had left was three saddle horses. The old sourdough neighbor who lived down the creek some few miles had carted Mark to his place before Judy left to make the rounds of the rodeos and was taking care of him and his horses.

There was still bills to pay and a winter to prepare for, so Judy had started out early that summer and for the first rodeo she could get to. She went from there, took on one after another and done well, but it takes money to live between rodeos and travel from one to another, and there was only a few times when she had a chance to take her chestnut with her for trick riding. Like with this last time, a horse buyer had come west and bought some horses around her country, and when he loaded to ship them east and there was room in one of the cars to slip in her horse, she tried to dicker with the buyer for that space. But there was no dickering, the horse buyer just handed her a pass to go and come back on and told her to go ahead and use the space for her horse. As good luck would have it the shipment of horses was going to the big town where she now was, and she could of stayed in the caboose if she'd wanted to but instead she stayed with her horse at one end of the car, and it was no wonder, Flint thought, that she was all in and hungry when she got to the big town and he found her.

But that whole summer had been pretty well just like that with her, she'd sent all the money she could to Mark, for his leg wound hadn't healed at all well and the doctor had to make a trip every once in a while to dress it. Mark wouldn't hear of no hospital, and it was feared for a spell that the leg would have to be amputated.

As it was now, Judy had just enough money to pay her entrance fee for the cowgirl bronc riding event, and as for eating and a place to stay during the rodeo, she thought she could get a little money in advance on her contract for trick riding. But Flint told her that she thought wrong and that this rodeo management wouldn't advance nothing on anything, not even loan her four bits even if she offered her horse as security, and that horse, for trick riding purposes, was worth five hundred dollars.

"You sure had it plenty tough," Flint said when she got thru, "and I know you need the money bad, but I wish you wouldn't enter in the bronc riding. You're too tired out now and maybe won't make anything out of it. I hear there's quite a few girls going to contest here this year, and good bronc riders too that you know.

"But, as I said before, we'll talk that over in the morning after you're well rested up and while we're having breakfast. Want any more to eat?" he asked. "I could eat a little something myself." But she only shook her head and smiled her thanks.

He stood up to leave, and as a "good night" he says, "Don't worry about that rawhide-bellied husband of yours, he'll be riding broncs again next year. A few hurts only makes us fellers good. It's all in the game."

XI
CHAMPION ALL-AROUND COWBOY

FLINT GOT UP at his usual early time the next morning, took down a couple of cups of black coffee, a cigarette with each, and went to the rodeo grounds and feeding pens where he again took care of Judy's horse, seen that the saddle and all was there and not been touched, talked to some of the boys for a spell and then went back to the hotel to wait until Judy got up and called him.

He waited in the lobby and for quite a while. Some of the cowboys came by and on their way out would stop and talk a while, some of 'em bronc riders that liked to see him but wished he hadn't come. First money would be hard to get with Flint to contest against.

He'd about made up his mind to call Judy's room and wake her up when a bell hop paged him. She was up and dressed and coming down, and by that time, Flint had quite an appetite, something he seldom had for breakfast. But it was past breakfast time now, near middle forenoon.

"Sure must of had a good rest," he thought, and as she appeared a little while later, dressed in town clothes, she sure looked like she had. He remarked about it, and she came back at him with saying that living on sandwiches she had the brakeman bring her, and sleeping in a stock car for the many days over the two thousand miles, was no way to get rest, pretty dimples or keep a wave. It would take her another day to get over that trip.

They went to the dining room, a good breakfast was brought on, and as it was well started, Flint again tried to talk her out of entering in bronc riding, but she only shook her head and smiled at him as she had the night before when he tried that.

"Remember what Mark once said at the cottonwood camp a couple of years ago," she says. "He said that we could never both lose and one of us would bring home the bacon. Well, it's up to me to do that this year, and even tho the trick riding contract will pay pretty good, I've got to make more, and that's where the bronc riding comes in.

"This will be my last rodeo for this year, then I'll be going home to take care of Mark, and being winter is coming on there'll

A good breakfast was brought on, and as it was well started
Flint again tried to talk her out of entering in bronc riding.

have to be a six month supply of grub stacked up on the shelves in the dugout cellar, clothes, medecines and other things for the house, because where our little ranch is located it's pretty hard to get to town and get anything. It's quite a ways, sixty miles, the snow gets deep and drifts bad. A blizzard might come out of a clear sky and blind and freeze you. Besides it's too cosy in our little loghouse to want to get out when the weather is bad, and good or bad I'll be wanting to take quite a rest when I get there, and I want to take home enough money so Mark and me can do that in comfort. You understand, Flint, and that's why I want to take on the bronc riding, in hopes that will bring me some more money and so we can do that."

Flint listened well and understood, and after a while he says: "You sure need a good long rest all right, Judy, but I've got a better idea than you coming out on fool broncs for that extra money. It always scares me to see a girl riding one of them, and you'd be doing me a big favor to let me stake you to the same amount the first prize would be and you keep off of 'em. You ain't in shape, and when you and Mark are riding again next year you can easy pay me back then or any time you wish, but do me a favor and leave the broncs alone."

In answer, Flint only received the same shake of the head and appreciating smile as before. So seeing there was no use pleading with her any more, and after the two finished their breakfast, they slowly walked to the grounds and rodeo headquarters. There Judy went over the trick riding contract with an official, and while she was doing that, Flint went to another official to do his entering and pay the fees for each event he entered in. He entered Judy in bronc riding first, while she was busy with the other official, and he paid her fee, then for himself he entered for saddle bronc riding, bull-dogging and steer roping. That was all and he was going to do better than his level best to win in all three.

Judy, hearing that Flint had paid her entrance fee, tried hard to get peeved at him, but she didn't get far, and "Nell's bells," Flint says, "you got to have something to eat on, get your clothes cleaned and other things." He grinned, "This is one time I got it on you and you can't do nothing about it."

"We'll see," she said, determined but smiling.

Most of the cowboys recognized Judy that day as her and Flint went to the feeding pens to look at her horse and around. All of them was glad to see her, for Judy was well liked by all who knew her, even the cowgirls. A few was there and at the sight of them Judy realized that Flint had been right. She'd have hard competition in the bronc riding, for it seemed like all of the best had gathered there for that rodeo, and there was a good many of 'em. But she put that off, saying to herself, the more the merrier, and with another good day's and long night's rest she'd be ready to compete with any of 'em. . . . Only thing was she wished her outfit wasn't so shabby looking, but the judges don't care much for that. Flint had now slipped into overalls and everyday shirt, shining up her chestnut's slick hide and brushing his mane. When he'd get thru that horse would detract a considerable from her shabby looking outfit.

She left Flint with the horse and the cowboys, and went to the hotel to do what she could with her clothes. She mended and patched the rest of the forenoon, until Flint called, a little after one o'clock and told her to come down, that it was time to eat again. But before she went down she had a bell-hop come get the clothes she had fixed, they was to be called for right away to be cleaned and pressed and returned that evening or before nine the next morning, in time to get dressed for the parade, as was required of every contestant to ride in.

They didn't eat at the hotel that noon, too much silverware, too many chandeliers and the atmosphere wasn't at all homey. So Flint took Judy out a ways to a place he knew and where grub was more to taste. Many cowboys was there at a long string of tables put together at their order, and Flint and Judy sat there to join 'em.

More rest and more cleaning up for Judy that afternoon and that night. Flint asked her to go to a show or some place with him but she refused, saying *her own* show started on the morrow and she wanted to be in shape for that.

And she sure seemed to be as she came down to meet Flint at breakfast early the next morning. That cowboy couldn't help but wonder as he seen her, a very different looking person from the dejected one he'd found sitting between the two horses a couple of days before, but them two days had sure done wonders with her.

"You sure must have powerful recuperating powers, Judy," Flint says to her as she came near.

"I guess I'll need 'em too for the next six days," she said, smiling.

Breakfast over with, they hit for the rodeo grounds again, where all the saddle horses was being given another grooming, braided manes and tails was let down and brushed to wavy, silky lengths. It was the day for the big parade, the only one there'd be, and to announce the grand opening of the rodeo. The parade was near a mile long when the time come, and all strung out and going along the best street of the big city where all traffic had been turned off during the time it took the Parade to go thru. It made a pretty sight for anybody's eye, from the shoeblack who rushed up from the side street, to the silk-hatted, monocled and spatted gentleman he crowded by to get a good look-see at the goings on.

The wide sidewalks was packed and could of hardly held another human all along the four miles the parade went, and the windows of the high priced shops was jammed about the same.

Flint in his dark blue shirt was riding well ahead and amongst the top contestants who was paired off with the cowgirls, but being there was only twelve cowgirls to over two hundred cowboys and others who rode that didn't go far, Flint might of lost Judy's company if he hadn't been right on the job and seen that he didn't. He'd shined up her saddle to go well with her well groomed horse, and her clothes being all fixed up, she didn't have to take any back seat from any of the other cowgirls now, not from a distance anyway.

"I'll be glad to get out of these streets and back to the grounds," says Flint as him and Judy rode along to the tune of the band. The whole parade flanked with crowds got on his nerves. "They think this is a wild west show or circus."

"It might be to them," says Judy, glancing at the many faces on both sides of the street, "but to us it's a case of having to pay to get here, pay to contest or perform, and pay to get back to where we come, if we win enough to be able to."

Back to the arena, and at two o'clock that afternoon the first day of the big contest started. With the grand entree, the band playing, all the contestants entering the arena and riding first in a big review circle, then in clover leaf shape and other ways, it made mighty colorful sight and much more impressive than could be seen in entrees of any bull fighting ring or arena. These contestants would be showing as much if not more skill as any good bull fighter ever could, and some of the events would be even more dangerous, only there'd be no helpless horses being gored or bulls being tortured and maddened to a final death. In our rodeos it's just the opposite, and the cowboy is the one that's most apt to be losing the blood, and sometimes his life.

That afternoon's contest, as with most all contests, opened with saddle bronc riding. Flint was fourth man up to ride, in the first bunch that was to be let out of the chutes, and that more than pleased him, for he craved action and he was ready.

He tried out a saddle as to stirrup length, then it was slipped over into the chute onto a creased and kinky back, cinched and Flint was perched on top of the chute ready to climb down into the rigging as he would be announced. At the first word of the announcer mentioning his name he was in the saddle and squeezing his legs in the tight place between the spooky outlaw's sides and the heavy chute timbers, to reach and get his feet in the stirrups. He didn't hear the announcer telling all about Flint Spears, the coming champion bronc rider, where he was from and so on. All he had ears for was the words "let's go" and see the chute gate opening.

As the words was heard and the chute gate opened, Flint's coming out was sure enough that of a coming champion, more like already one, and with both spurs up high along the horse's neck. On that horse, which was plenty tough, he was like a kid that'd been kept in a dark room for a long time, expecting a good licking as a wind up, and instead was handed a ticket to the ball game and some change for "pop."

He was having the time of his life on that crooked, hard hitting horse, spurs araking from neck to hip at every jump, and he didn't know he'd finished his ride until a pick-up man rode alongside of him and took the braided rope bucking rein out of his hand and snubbed the bucking horse's head up. Flint slid off of him, dodged an expected kick and hit back for the chutes. He felt like he could of took on ten more such horses straight hand running right then.

As he went along the tall fence towards the chutes he came to Judy who'd closely watched him ride. Her eyes was shining with pleasure as she says, "Do you know that was a final horse* you just rode? And what a ride you put up on him. I wish poor old Mark would of been here to see it."

"So do I," says Flint, with a cheerful grin. "He will be again."

Along with her trick riding which was for every day, Judy was up to ride a bucking horse that day, too. She was near as anxious to get at him and out of the chute as Flint had been with his. She put up a good ride, as good as any of the other cowgirls who rode that day and better than most of 'em. Her head didn't bob and she kept asmiling, confident all thru the ride.

Flint hated to look at her riding, but being it was Judy, he couldn't help it, and he was glad when the ride was over and she was picked up off her horse.

Events after events followed, there was no waiting from one to the other, and nothing was done at any snail's pace, it was all with plenty of action and speed. Then come the bull-dogging, with good fresh and wiry longhorn steers, and Flint was up for that event for that day also. But as he wanted action that was fine with him, and

*The hardest ones and used for final decision on championships.

here was some more. He built to that steer like he was starving for raw meat on the hoof and was going to eat him up, and he done good time on the tough-necked one, better than the average.

He now was done for the day, so was Judy, he wouldn't be riding nor bull-dogging on the next day and was up for steer roping only. Judy wouldn't be riding a bronc either on the next day, there'd be only her regular trick riding along with the others in that exhibition. Flint was glad for that.

When the next day come and the afternoon contest started and went on, Flint and Judy had plenty of time to visit around with the contestants, Judy with the cowgirls in a special box for them by the band, and Flint most everywhere in the arena. They had plenty of time to watch the goings on, and Flint was perticularly in watching the events he'd entered in. He was glad when the steer roping event come and so he could get into action, and having watched for the best rope horse the day before, he'd rented him from the cowboy owner for the short time he'd be needing him in that event, and he had him saddled and ready when his time come to rope his steer.

The horse was good and fast and took Flint to his steer in great shape. He made a good catch, throwed the slack of his rope over the steer's rump, and riding by him at top speed, lifted that steer to land so hard and lay so still that there wasn't a quiver in him. He'd slipped off his horse before the steer had landed and in the wink of an eye had him tied down.

Flint didn't know it until that evening, at headquarters, when horses was drawed for the next afternoon's contest, day moneys was handed out for different events of that day and time was checked up on roping and bull-dogging, that he'd broke all records by two seconds in steer roping that afternoon, all previous and present records.... There never was a more surprised cowboy no time than Flint was right then, for that was the last event he'd ever expected to win in. He'd felt lucky if he'd only made good enough time so his name wouldn't be scratched out of that event, and now he wouldn't give himself credit. He just had a lucky break all the way thru he told himself and others, it was only an accident he made that record breaking time, and he was sure he couldn't repeat.

But here he was, having a mighty good chance to hold the championship in steer roping to the end of that rodeo. He'd already won that in bull-dogging and that made him want to laugh, for he'd always figured that if he ever won any championship it would be in the saddle bronc riding. First anyway, and *maybe* in the other events afterwards, a long time afterwards.

And now he was more than ever determined to win that saddle bronc riding championship. That would cover all he'd aimed to do and more. His ambition of many years of hard contesting would then be more than he'd realize.

So, when come the day and time for Flint to ride in the semi-finals, and he came out on a spinning sidewinder, one of the hardest kind of buckers there is to ride, he was full of that ambition. He rode wild and reckless and never once looked down his horse's bowed head. That in itself was sure some feat, for such kind of buckers are mighty hard to keep track of even if the rider watches close and knows three or four jumps ahead which way he was going to go, which is of course as impossible as guessing where we go when we evaporate from this planet.

Flint didn't have to ride long before the judges called it *a ride*, and he was enjoying himself when he was surprised by the pick-up man riding alongside of him and wanting the bucking rein to pull the horse's head up. Flint grinned and remarked afterwards that it was the shortest ride he ever put up.

"Yep," says one of the contestants, "but it was sure a wampus of a one, and as wild as it was short. You made the finals in the first four jumps alone."

Judy rode another bucker that day too and it looked to Flint that she'd topped the other cowgirl riders. Anyway she made the finals and was high enough in points so she had a mighty good chance for first. Another such a ride on another as good a horse and Flint felt pretty sure she'd make it.

It'd been a great day for the two, so was the day following when Flint, to his surprise again, made second best time in steer roping and ranked third in bulldogging.

The day of the finals come, Flint easy rode his horse, and with very few riders now left in the bucking contest, he made the grand finals. The grand final rides would be made at the very last of that last and same day's contest, after which the winners of the main events would be announced.

All was going mighty well, *too well to last,* Flint thought. Here all thru this contest he hadn't a scratch nor a bruise, not even a bump that his bum leg usually got, and before any other part of him would. He'd been strutting around, feeling like a two year old, and it was no wonder, because he about the same as had the first money for bronc riding in his pocket. He was pretty sure about the steer roping too because with the last and third steer he'd roped, he again made near as good as he had with the first. As to the bull-dogging he wasn't so sure, but he'd already had the championship there and that record would have to be beat before another champion could be declared and recognized as such.

Flint was sitting on a sawdust-filled sack against the Arena fence, feeling like a lark in thinking of the prospects ahead, when Judy came and sat by him.

"You sure made a good ride on that final horse, Flint," she says. "Far as that goes they was all mighty good and by far the best I've ever seen in any contest."

Judy kind of talked dull and as tho it was an effort for her to say what she did. She sure had been more lively and sparkling the few days before, and up to the last time he talked to her just a couple of hours past. It made him wonder, and looking at her he had to ask:

"What's the matter, Judy, don't you feel well?"

She smiled a little, and looking away acrost the arena, she says, "Oh, I feel all right, I guess."

"You guess?" says Flint, surprised. "Why, you ought to feel all right, or you'd better. You're sitting high in points for first in bronc riding, and now that you're up so well you've got to *ride*, ride for yours and Mark's sake and bring home the bacon. You'll be riding for the finals pretty soon now, and from the girls that's left to compete against you, it sure looks like you're going to make it. . . . You should feel all perked up, Judy."

The girl sat by him for quite a spell without saying anything, and hardly listening to the cheering talk Flint was putting on. Cowboys came by to stop and crack a few jokes, then as the cowgirl bronc riding event for the finals drew near, there was a few of 'em came by to stop and talk a spell. But Judy didn't seem to hardly see or hear any of them. She kept astaring acrost the arena and then down to the ground, and Flint, watching her, was sort of worried.

Finally, when none other was around she asked him, "You've had plenty of hunches, haven't you, Flint?"

"Why sure," he says, wondering. "I guess everybody has.

"Did you ever go by 'em?"

"A few times, and when I did I most always wished I hadn't; there was nothing to 'em."

"But there might of been if you hadn't followed 'em. With women I think hunches are stronger; besides, we have intuition, which is something men lack."

"Yes, I heard about that," Flint says, then he squinted at her. "But what are you getting at anyhow, Judy? Is it that you have a hunch you won't make the finals? If that's it, you better get that out of your mind and get that old riding spirit of yours there instead. The spirit to win."

"It's not that," Judy said.

"Is it Mark?"

"No."

"Well, what in samhill is it then?"

Judy only shrugged her shoulders, smiled and didn't answer.

The horses for the cowgirls' bronc riding contest was being hazed into the chutes while the relay race and other track events was going on. Judy got up to see as to the stirrup length of the committee saddle she was to use, and to the saddling of the horse she'd drawed. There was no grand finals in the cowgirls' bronc riding and if she

191

rode this horse well, and he bucked good enough, it was near a cinch that she'd win first, or at least second prize.

The saddling done and everything all ready, there was a little waiting to do until the track events was over, then being she'd have to wait some more until she was called she went to sit by Flint again, not saying a word, just vacant gazing acrost the Arena.

"Better pull yourself together, Judy, and forget whatever seems to be getting you down. This is your last ride to win and you better make it good."

"Yes, Flint, this is going to be my very last ride and for all time. I feel it."

The way she said that sent a shiver running along his backbone. "You're not afraid of the horse, are you?" he asks.

"No. He's just the same as any of the others to me."

All puzzled and sort of worried, the thought that'd come to Flint a little while back, that "all was going mighty well, too well to last," returned to his mind again. Maybe that was a hunch, the hunch Judy had spoke of, and thinking of that made him sort of stargaze acrost the arena, too.

But there's nothing to that, he kept saying to himself, Judy most likely only felt a little tense or maybe had a case of the blues in missing Mark so.

The track events over with, the judges, pick-up men and all that belonged near the chutes returned. One cowgirl was sliding into the saddle and soon the contest for the cowgirl finals was started. The first cowgirl came out and done a pretty fair ride, but, Flint says to Judy, "You can sure beat that." He loaned her his shaps.

A couple more cowgirls came out and done well, and by that time Judy had sort of snapped out of her trance and come to life again. She talked natural and laughed a little, and when come her time to ride she patted Flint on the hand, smiled at him and went towards the chutes like the good one she was.

Flint stood up, feeling mighty relieved. "She'll bring the money home," he thought.

The chute gate opened, the horse made three easy jumps as he came out, and then all at once he lit into it for fair, not at all like a cowgirl's bucking horse but more like the ones that's handed to the top contestants for the grand finals. He was crooked, high, and as hard hitting as any of them and acted like he might fall over backwards any time between jumps. That horse made Flint wonder if one of them final horses hadn't been slipped in the chute by mistake.

Judy was riding, but on such a horse she couldn't ride like she had on the others. Her head began to bob at the first hard jump that horse made, then with the next few jumps she got limp, limp as a rag. It was a great wonder she stuck, Flint thought, and he knew then that she was near unconscious.

Realizing that, he run towards the pick-up men and hollered at 'em, "Pick her up. Pick her up, you dumb fools; can't you see she's unconscious?"

But they was quite a ways off and before they could get to her the horse made a powerful high jump in the air and shook Judy off of him up there with a hard kicking buck. Before she hit the ground he struck her on the side of the head with a front hoof and it made a smashing sound that could be heard even as far as where Flint was. That hard blow stood her on her head, and as the outlaw horse went by he kicked her in the side and sent her spinning to crumble to the ground. Everyone in the arena figured she was killed with that first blow on the side of the head and dead before she hit the ground. . . . She'd been right in her hunch that it would be her last ride.

That tragic happening stopped the whole contest goings on for a spell, until the ready ambulance speeded in the area and took her away, not to the hospital, the doctor said, but to the undertakers, and Flint, having a couple of hours before his time for the grand final ride, went along, and giving instructions as to what to do with the body, to be shipped to the ranch, he went back to the rodeo grounds, sure not the same Flint of a couple of hours before. He was now the one who went around in a trance, or daze.

But instead of that getting him down it helped him when come time for his grand final ride. He was mad and hurt clear thru and a good tough and ornery bronc would be just the medicine for him, something to sort of loosen up his feelings on, and the tougher and wickeder the bronc the better.

He came out of the chute on just such a one, and now he was near happy to find that out as he went to work on him. It would of been just too bad if he'd drawed only an average bucker right then, too bad for the horse and everybody around. As it was, that horse made it interesting for him, and the ride that cowboy put up near

As the outlaw horse went by he kicked her in the side
and sent her spinning to crumble to the ground.

made the judges', the other contestants' and the audiences's eyes pop in wonder. Flint didn't lose his head in that ride, and on that hard twister he showed such skill and fine points that had never been witnessed before, by judges and contestants who'd seen thousands of good rides. With that, Flint seemed to take the hard twists and jolts as easy as if he'd been paddling along in a canoe on a quiet lake. He was going to make this ride one that would be remembered by all present, and at the same time sort of even up for Judy by making a fool out of the worse horse in that bucking string, which also had the reputation of being the worse horse any contestant ever tried to ride. The horse was well known at every rodeo he was taken to, and helped draw crowds a considerable, for he was a big lead star amongst the tough ones.

Admiring the sight of that ride so, the judges near forgot to call it to an end, a pick-up man finally got 'em out of their trance, and as he rode and got the bucking rein, Flint slid off and, with the ease of a cat, landed on his feet and walked away as cool and unflustered looking as tho he'd just stepped off a merry go 'round.

The rest of the grand final riders done well, and soon as all had rode, and being it was the last day of the rodeo the points on bronc riding and time on bull-dogging and roping had been checked up on with every event of that day as it went, added along with points and time of the days before, and winners decided on amongst the judges after each event, it didn't take no time for the winners and champions of all events to be lined up in the arena, in front of the most important crowd in the grandstand and there to be announced.

Flint was first and foremost in line, and now, after being thru with his ride, he was again in a sort of a daze. He hardly heard his name mentioned nor any of the fine things that was being said about him and of his skill as a rider, roper and bull-dogger, and he didn't come to himself much until it was announced that with all the points that'd stacked up in his favor from first prize winnings at other rodeos, and now winning first prize at this one, he was declared champion saddle bronc rider.

That pleased him to full awakening, but that wasn't all. He was also declared champion steer roper and bull-dogger, and right there in front of the crowded grandstand he was handed a gold flowered silver cup which reached from his elbow to above his hat brim, with the figure of a bucking horse and rider on top and engraved writing on the side which read "For All-Around Cowboy Championship."

XII

ALL FOR ONE, ONE FOR ALL

T HAD BEEN Flint's intentions to hit back for the ∿ after the big rodeo was over and take on a few winter contests in that southern country. But now, with Judy's going he felt the place he should go was to Mark's, in the northern ranges, and see to that cowboy until he sort of got over the shock from the tragic happening which he'd sooner or later hear of.

He received his prize moneys, which now made quite a sum. Then, as Judy had fulfilled her contract on trick riding he collected that, also three mount moneys for three times she rode in the bucking contest. As to her saddle and outfit, he boxed that up with his silver trophy and another prize saddle that'd been presented him and shipped it all. The chestnut would be in a carload of roping and bull-dogging horses, along with the carloads of bucking horses and steers that'd be shipped back west to winter.

Flint took a fast train and in the baggage car of that same train was a covered casket carrying Judy's resting body. The three day trip west was anything but a cheerful one for Flint. He kept athinking about breaking the tragic news to Mark and how that cowboy would take it. That would be near as hard to take as the witnessing of the happening, and worse in a way, because he figured it'd be months and maybe years before the hurt would heal. It wouldn't be so bad if he was up and working, but sitting in a wheel chair most all day along and just grieving would make it plenty tough.

Thinking of all them things as the train rolled along sure took away the great feeling and joy of the successful summer Flint'd had, of being acknowledged Champion all-around cowboy, that mighty hard to reach goal accomplished. And, but for the happening of a couple of days before he would of felt proud and happy all over. He could still see that bucker's smashing front hoof and hear the sound when it connected. Then again would come the thought of breaking the news to Mark, and Flint sort of pictured him, all crushed for days and then weeks and months of grieving. With such steady thinking on the subject sometimes made Flint shake himself, get up and pace up and down in the smoker or go sit in the observation car, outside, and try to interest himself in the country he rode thru. It was only then that he could get his mind on the past summer's doings and great wind up, and then, for short spells, he would feel satisfied and happy.

He was glad when at last he reached the little cow town where he was to get off, for he felt that as soon as Mark was told, which was going to be mighty hard to do, he'd be relieved considerable, and as misery likes company that would help some too. He'd be keeping Mark company and doing other things.

Flint lit in the little cow town about the middle forenoon, hunted up and hired a driver to take him out in a car, and with good driving on the rough roads he got to the sourdough's ranch just as that feller was fixing dinner.

There's no telling of the glad surprise that was on Mark's face as Flint walked into the one big-roomed log house, and at that he seen that Mark hadn't heard or been notified as yet. But that time was soon to come, after the noon meal was over and digested. Mark still used his wheel chair.

Cheerful talk went on during the meal, Mark hungry for news, and the sourdough, altho hungry for food, was also interested. Any news came a long time between out there, and strange as it might be was always welcome. Then, and as was expected, there was questions about Judy, how was she, when would she be back and how did she make out, to all of which Flint only answered, that she could be here at the ranch most any day (her casket had been left at a funeral home in town), her horse was being shipped back with a load of rope horses, and yes, she'd done fine at the rodeo, up to the last day.

Mark didn't catch the "up to the last day" and Flint was glad. That would hold for a while.

It was a fine warm and sunny afternoon, and that was good, for a gloomy rainy or snowy day which that northern country usually gets at that time of the year would of made things worse along with the sad job Flint had to do that afternoon. The more he thought of it the more he wanted to get it over with, and the sooner the better. But he waited and helped clear the table and wiped the dishes. There was a few cigarettes rolled and smoked during more talk, and then, after the sourdough went outside and Flint seen him start for an afternoon's ride he stood up, walked around a bit and then, his jaw clamped, he came to a stop before Mark and said between his teeth.

"Prepare yourself for bad news, cowboy. You've rode plenty of tough horses but this is tougher than all of that put together. Don't let it get you down."

At that he handed him a piece he'd clipped out of a newspaper of the city where the rodeo had been held. It told plain and in a few words of the tragedy and Judy's sudden death, how it happened and all.

Mark read it once and twice without showing much concern, then he looked up at Flint and sort of smiled, unbelieving. "Why this can't mean Judy, my Judy?" he says.

"You've rode plenty of tough horses but this is tougher than all of that put together."

"Yes, Mark, it is," says Flint, standing firm and trying hard not to show his feelings. "I was with her most of the time during the rodeo and wasn't so far from her when I seen it happen."

For days Mark sat in his wheel chair and like in a stupor. Black coffee and cigarettes is all he'd have, and if talked to, he hardly seemed to hear, and there was seldom an answer. It was a sad house for the sourdough and Flint for a while, and the two sometimes talking it over as to what to do always wound up with throwing up their hands. There was nothing a doctor or anybody could do, the hurt would have to wear itself out.

Then one day, like out of a clear sky, Mark came to life, begin to show interest and talk, and that day he got up from his wheel chair and waddling around on account of his one short leg acted like he wanted to get busy at something. He couldn't do much, he said, only maybe set the table, wash dishes and other such few chores around in the house, but he wanted to do something, anything that he could.

"I remember you telling me," he said to Flint, "that I shouldn't let it get me down. I got to thinking about that most all last night. Judy would feel bad if I would, and I've made up my mind to come out of it. I'll be contesting again next year, Flint. I won't be able to take on bronc riding or bull-dogging no more I don't think, but my rope arm is still good and I can go after steer roping and such like."

"That's the spirit, cowboy," said the surprised and pleased Flint. "You'll be as good as new by the time spring comes."

It was during that same day that Mark said, "I sure must of been sort of out of my head aplenty the last few days, Flint, because I never thought of asking you. . . Where is Judy's b-body?"

"At the funeral home in town. I didn't know where you wanted to lay it to rest and couldn't ask you while you was in such a stupor. I'm sure glad you're out of it now"

Mark thought a short while and then said, "There's only one place where I'd have her rest, a place she always liked and where we used to sit of evenings. It's on a knoll by the house on our ranch. There's a big old lone juniper tree there, with a carpet of creeping cedar under it, and that's the place where I want her, under the shade and shelter of that juniper and thick carpet of the evergreen creeping cedar covering her. Let's go to town and get her, Flint. We'll take the long democrat buggy of Regal's, it'll be easier riding for her."

So it was that, early the next morning when a light and the best of Regal's, the sourdough's, good teams was hooked onto the democrat and headed for town. Going and coming it took four days for the trip and the democrat was well loaded on the way back. Alongside of the covered casket was the big box of saddles Flint had shipped, Judy's being one of them. Then a preacher to do the ceremony of burial had been brought along and riding on the seat beside Flint. Mark was in the back, beside the coffin. He'd slid the top partition so he could look at her face thru the little square. Flint had seen to it that the embalming work would be of the best, and now she still looked very near lifelike and as tho she was only sleeping. She was even smiling a little like all was peaceful.

Mark's eyes was sort of glued on her pretty face most of the time on the way. He'd mumble and talk to her and once in a while there'd be choking sobs. When he would raise his eyes it would be to look at the chestnut that was being led at the back of the rig and no time tightening on the lead rope. That faithful horse had packed Judy thru many good trick rides, and now he was the only living thing that would keep reminding him of her.

Back to Mark's ranch and at the top of the knoll where Judy's casket would be buried, the chestnut, groomed and shining, was saddled with her saddle and was present for the burial, Mark leaning on his neck while the preacher done the services, and steady looking at her face thru the little square in the casket as the preacher's chant and prayers went on.

Flint and Regal stood by with bared heads all the while and looking mighty solemn. Not a whimper came from Mark's bowed head, not even when the casket was lowered into the grave with ropes. She looked so restful, and that little hint of a smile so peaceful.

It wasn't until the shutter was closed on the black casket and Flint and Regal eased down the first few shovelfuls of earth to cover it and starting to fill the grave, that Mark covered his face with his hands, slowly sat down, and tears begin trickling thru his fingers. The chestnut standing by him seemed to realize what was going on (some horses do realize, or seem to feel considerable more than lots of humans). His head was bowed, looking into the grave being filled, and every once in a while he'd nozzle Mark's shoulder or bared head, like in sympathy.

The chestnut standing by him seemed to realize and sympathize.

After the first few shovelfuls, and while Mark kept his face covered, Flint and Regal more than went at it in finishing filling the grave. It wasn't a pleasant job, then the thick matting of creeping cedar which had been uprooted and layed back like a thick green blanket was carefully replanted to cover the grave and to spread on. At the head of the shaded grave was planted a thick and wide slab which Regal had hewed out of a heavy and seasoned juniper while Flint and Mark had gone to town. He'd figured that Mark wouldn't want no marble nor granite for the monument. Too dead and cold looking. On the slab, and with a redhot iron, he'd seared deep the simple wording: JUDY—THE FAIREST, AND WINNER TO HER LAST RIDE. Then only the dates of her birth and death, without mention of the words.

Mark looked at the juniper slab for a long time, at the green carpet of creeping cedar covering the grave. Then, even as heavy hearted as he was he turned to Regal and Flint and his moist eyes showed more than a glint of appreciation.

"It all makes me feel she's still alive," he finally said.

"Yes," the preacher said to that. "Her spirit is and will always be with you."

With feeling that Judy was now near him always, Mark livened up to where he was more his old self and would even laugh some as Flint told of funny happenings since he'd seen him last. There was reminiscing of the days when the two rode for the 45 and the ～ and contested together.

Flint's company was a great help to Mark and he recuperated fast in all his hurts. Then one day, in the dead of winter, Mark was for moving back to his own ranch, remarking that he'd caused Regal enough extra work and trouble. He could manage well enough now, he said, and besides he wanted to be near Judy. He didn't say grave.

But Regal reared up at that and landed on Mark with a fair cussing and talking-to. "Why you dumfool," he said, during the talking-to he gave him. "You couldn't even pack in chips to start a fire with, let alone cutting wood, chopping it and packing it in." He wound up by saying, "And now that I'm used to having your useless carcass around, don't you think it'll be lonesome here if you go?"

Mark and Flint had to grin during the talking-to, and finally, when Regal sort of run out of breath and stopped, all was quiet for a spell, like the quiet after a thunder storm, and then Mark spoke up.

"Well, I'll tell you what you do, then," he says. "You move over to my place. I've got a better house, stable and corrals than you have, your horses run on my range as much as they do your own, and you can ride watch on them from there as well as you can from here. And being you keep up only one or two horses at the time, you could haul a jag of hay for them once in a while. Besides," he added on as a wind up, "I won't be able to make use of my place, not until I get some cattle again, and it will be quite a while before I can do that, so being my place joins yours and your horses run in my country as well as yours, why not use it in connection?"

That quieted Regal and set him to thinking. He thought on it for a couple of days and then on the second evening, he blurted out with, "I think you're right, Mark. I could use your fenced land and maybe later on get a bunch of cattle to run on your range and winter on your place. I could run 'em with you on shares and start you in cattle again that way."

Well, that was more than Mark could have expected, and he right away seen where it was a good proposition, for Regal as well as for himself. For many years Regal had made his living out of raising horses. The only cows he had on the ranch was the "contented" kind in labeled cans, and as there wasn't much riding and care with horses, being out on the range the year around and no hay to put up, only for the saddle horses he kept up of winters, he'd have plenty of time to run and take care of a little bunch of cattle on the side, using Mark's place. Later on Mark could maybe ride again and help him that way.

Mark had no suspicion but Regal's deciding to move over to his place and use his land was altogether to help Mark, help him get started in the cattle business again, and that way keep him in interest and to better forget his sorrow. As for himself he didn't need no cattle. He had plenty of money stored away and drawing interest, and even tho he had only a couple of hundred head of horses, they was good horses, and he sold enough halter-broke (broke to lead) geldings in one year to keep him all he ever wanted for five years.

But he wouldn't lose Mark now, as he'd said, he was used to having him around, and just the thought of helping him without his knowing pleased him even more than it did Mark to moving back to his ranch, even along with cattle running there again, on shares, but Mark only thought of that as a mighty good business proposition, and that was helping Regal also. He had no idea that Regal had any money or that he was making much out of his horses.

The moving being decided on and the next morning come, it was hard to keep Mark from getting around and doing too much, such as lifting and packing things, and a couple of times, Regal threatened to tie him down to his chair if he didn't quit.

"I don't want to have to take you to the hospital or go get a doctor to come out here again," he bellered at him once, "and besides, you're only in the way anyhow. You go twiddle your thumbs. Flint and me'll take care of this moving."

Mark let that go by with a grin, but the talking-to did slow him down some and he seen where Regal was right. The mention of the hospital alone was enough to stop him. He'd rather went to jail.

There wasn't so much to move, only the grub and bedding and a few pet kettles and things that Regal wanted to take along. There was already plenty of kettles and things at Mark's house. The place had been left with all furniture, dishes, curtains, pictures and fixings just as Judy had left it. Flint thought of that before the moving was decided on and wondered how that would affect Mark, if all that was in the cosy three room log house, as Judy had left it, wouldn't remind him too much of her and make him miss her so as to make him go mad.

Everything that Regal wanted to take, along with Mark's bedding and things, and Flint's stuff, went in one wagon load and was ready to be hauled out long before noon come. Regal then saddled up, run a team in from a tall grass pasture, and Flint was down at the corrals to help harness and then hook 'em to the wagon. Regal took another look around inside the house, closed the door and hopped on the seat beside Flint. Mark was in the back on some bedding.

Regal released the brake and started the team, when Mark spoke up and, grinning, says. "Ain't you forgot something, Regal?"

Regal stopped his team, looked all over the back of the wagon then at the grinning Mark. "It's about the most important thing," he said. "Better go back in the house and take another look-see."

Handing the lines to Flint, Regal went back, and in a short while returned carrying the sourdough crock. There was a half peeved and sheepish look in his face as he carefully set the crock in the wagon.

Flint's wondering and worrying as to how it would affect Mark in again being in the house where him and Judy had been so happy, with everything around, some of which had been made by her own hands to steady remind him of her, had been of no use, for, instead Mark seemed near happy and at least more contented than he'd been at Regal's place.

The chestnut had been brought over and fed hay along with Regal's saddle horse. He wanted him close so he could see him, talk to him, and feel of his hide once in a while. Judy's saddle and whole outfit was brought into the house and hung up in one corner of the living room, Regal had spread out his bed in another corner. Many good pictures of her was dug up and tacked on' the walls of the bed room and living room.

"Near makes a feller feel like she's here, with all these pictures of her," says Regal to Flint one day as Mark was moseying around outside and near the chestnut.

Mark had been doing quite a bit of such moseying around since he'd been back to his home. Once in a while, with the help of a split willow crutch, he'd make it thru the snow up the knoll to the big juniper and the grave under it. He'd act pretty dull for quite a spell after every such visit, and Regal noticing that, told him he'd better cut out doing so much walking around outside or he'd hobble and side-line him to the stove.

Time had got to dragging pretty much for Flint. He was so used to action, and to have nothing to do was plain misery. He tried not to show any such signs, but Mark had noticed 'em, and one day, while Regal was out riding, he told him.

"There'll be some good rodeos pulled off south in another month or so, Flint, and I know you'll want to take 'em on and limber up at the old $\sim$ a while before you do. So if you want to go, don't stay here on my account. You've done a plenty more for me than I could ever repay in any way and I sure don't want to be more obliged to you by keeping you from what you want to do."

Flint was surprised but didn't blink an eye as he listened. Mark went on: "I can get around pretty good now, and I'll sure be all right with Regal on the job to see I don't do any fool stunts. I feel a lot better since I've been home too, and maybe it's because it seems as tho Judy is near me all the time, sometimes like I could near touch her when I close my eyes. . . . Yes, Flint, I'm all right now."

There wasn't much Flint could say, and there sure wasn't any more he could do. So a couple of days later, when the stage would be coming by to within half a day's drive, by team, was the time set for Flint's going.

The evening before that day come, Flint dug into the box he'd shipped Judy's and his prize saddle in, got out the tall burlap-wrapped silver trophy, unwrapped and set it on the living room table, saying: "I wish you'd keep this for me, Mark. I have no place to put it, and I think it's kind of pretty. If you run short of flour any time you go ahead and sell it. It's supposed to be worth a thousand dollars."

Mark hardly believed his eyes at the sight of the tall, shiny gold and silver ornamented cup, and when he came close and read the engraved wording on the side, "For all around cowboy championship," he was again more surprised, and in wonder he turned to Flint. Words near failed him but he finally managed to say:

"You son of a sea cook. . . . Why didn't you show me this before, or tell me while I was sort of out of my head? It would sure of helped bring me to."

"I thought of it but I was afraid it'd get you to pine to be around and contesting again."

"Yes, it might of maybe then at that. But not now no more, because I think I'll just stay here, by Judy and with Regal and raise cows again. I don't think I'll ever contest any more. . . . But," he went on, laying his hand on Flint's shoulder, "with you you're on the very top, top of 'em all, and I sure want to congratulate you, Flint. Stay there a long time, cowboy, and don't let me keep you away."

Hearing the louder than usual talk from the kitchen, Regal came out and, spotting the trophy, came to have a close look at it. But he didn't appreciate what the winning of that trophy really meant, or what a contestant had to go thru to win such a one. He'd never contested. He'd seen but only a few of the close and little rodeos.

"Sure a right pretty thing," he says, admiring it for its beauty alone. Then after a while he asked, "But what's it for? What do you keep in it?"

Flint grinned. "Raise the lid off it, Mark," he says. "Reach down inside and show him."

Mark did, and to his surprise as well as Regal's his hand come out full of ten, twenty and fifty dollar bills, all together amounting to quite a few hundred dollars. Mark looked at Flint for some sort of explanation.

"Judy's winnings," said Flint, serious.

The three was still, and Mark was staring at the money when Regal broke the spell. "I see now," he says. "The idea is to get that silver kettle filled with the stuff. Goshomighty, and by the size of it a man would have to rob a couple of banks to be able to do that."

Then, carrying on, to detract Mark, from Judy's last winnings, Flint showed 'em the fancy, hand-carved, silver-mounted saddle, another trophy. There was the same engraving as was on the cup, on a big silver place at the back of the cantle. It was a mighty pretty saddle to look at, and it drawed some more admiration.

"I'd leave it with you fellers," Flint says, "but it hasn't got the tree either of you would like, so I thought I'd take it south and sell it. My old regular saddle is at the ∿ where I'm going to be heading for."

It was mighty cold when early the next morning the team was hooked up and Flint was ready to start out. "Golly," he says, getting a last warming up by the stove. "I'm glad I'm going south or I'd sure have to buy me some heavy underwear and all such stuff to winter here with."

"Wish I was going with you, Flint," says Mark, in a sort of peaked voice, "and still I guess I don't. I'll sure miss you, old boy, but I've always missed you. I'll make the best of that too, and as you told me, I won't let it get me down."

The two shook hands, just said "So long. Take care of yourself," and Flint got in the democrat seat alongside of Regal, headed south, for more contests and conquests.

XIII
THE SQUAREST GAME

THE OLD ~ outfit was again mighty glad to see Flint. All, from the superintendent to the cook's flunky, was more than ever proud of him. They'd read in the papers of his winning the all-around cowboy championship and winnings at many other contests long before, and been looking for him back, sort of worried if he'd ever come back. And when he finally did, the superintendent and cow foreman showed their appreciation and joy at his return by turning over to him more and rougher horses which had accumulated in number while he was gone. He could go to work on 'em any time.

They figured that would please him a heap more than if he'd been offered the foreman's job and wages and top best cow horses, and they'd figured right, for Flint, after the long idle spell and grief he'd went thru and witnessed, didn't waste no time going to work on the rough ones.

He had a couple of weeks to limber up on 'em before the first rodeo he was going to take on for that year, and that was enough. The first one was one of Hurst's, and he came out of it winner in both saddle and bareback bronc riding. He made third money in steer roping and none in bull-dogging but he was still plenty high

*The superintendent and cow foreman showed their appreciation and
joy at his return by turning over to him more and rougher horses.*

in points from the rodeos of the years before to easy hold his
championship in them two events.

He done about the same at another rodeo, only a little better, by
winning second in bull-dogging. Flint hadn't as yet found his stride
for that year, only in bronc riding.

After them two contests there come quite a spell when there
was no rodeos he figured worth while going to, so, with a rough
string of ⌇ horses he went to work with the boys on the range
again. He wanted to unlimber his rope arm, along with keeping
limbered up with his riding.

Outside of bruises, loss of skin and strained muscles, Flint was
in fine shape to get into contesting game for fair that year. No rodeo

bronc could be much if any worse than the ∿ horses he'd been riding, and even roping off of, which was plenty dangerous, and when he received notice of a good rodeo paying big moneys, he bid the outfit good-bye for a spell and went, every one and all wishing him the best, and not to forget to come back.

The rodeo was to the north, only a few hundred miles west of Mark's ranch. Flint had never contested there before, but as contestants go and make the good ones he knew the most of them that'd come, and to his glad surprise he run into Mike Ryan there. Hadn't seen him for three years, and now Mike had six of the best roping and "dogging" horses in the game, which he'd done well by renting to contestants for use in them events. He'd done fair in contesting in them same events besides and kind of looked prosperous, also a little stockier.

The two, not having seen one another for so long, had quite a bit to talk about. The spell of calamity that'd landed on Mark and Judy was brought up and talked over, and while on such subject, Mike said that he got off pretty lucky, considering. He'd only got three broken ribs one time and a broken ankle another time, both of the happenings in bull-dogging, the first after he'd got his steer down, that steer raising his head and slamming it against Mike's ribs in trying to get up. The second was in clamping his boot heels into the ground while bracing himself in stopping his steer to throw him.

"But, as good luck would have it," he went on to say, "both of them breaks happened during stretches when there was no rodeos going on much and I needed a rest each time I got it."

"I got off luckier than that," Flint grinned. "Only a dislocated knee cap and such like."

"That's not surprising," says Mike. "You have a knack of seeing things coming before they even start."

Mike, like with all the other contestants, had heard and read of Flint's steady winnings all over the country for the past years, and it wasn't anything new when he finally heard of him winning the all around championship.

"Keep it up, old boy," he said to that. "I'm betting you'll be knocking 'em for a loop again this year."

"I'm going to try to," says Flint.

And Flint come near doing just that. . . . If it was heard that he'd be at this or that contest, many good first prize winning contestants went to other ones. There was of course many contestants who figured themselves as good, and tried to raise the ante over him on points. Different ones did get first prize winnings over him, but the horses Flint drawed would be to blame for that, didn't buck hard enough so that cowboy could make a showing, and just good enough so he wouldn't be allowed a reride. But he drew many top buckers at good big contests, and then no other contestants had any chance with him, not that year. And that fall, to cap things off in good shape and keep him well in the lead as still all around champion cowboy he won the world championship in bronc riding.

When he went back to his winter range, the old ⌒⌒, he had another trophy and prize saddle to take along with him. That saddle, being made on a roper tree and good for all around range work, he gave to an old cowboy who always thought that Flint was, not *one of* the best, but the *very* best hand that ever straddled a horse, and in his seventy odd years he'd seen many.

That old cowboy had his own saddle wore down thru in some parts, wore thin and patched in many other parts and it was about ready to fall apart. The foreman had told him just a few days before that a jerk of the rope from one more good calf would do that for him.

So, when Flint gave him the new prize saddle, no silver on that one, that old hand was plumb dumbfounded, not so much for the saddle itself which was "just the very kind he'd long wanted," it was that it was given to him and by none other than Flint Spears. . . . From then on there was no prouder cowboy on that outfit nor any-where else, and he hardly thought of the fact that now he wouldn't have to hold out on his next month's wages which he sent the most part of to his widowed daughter every month so she could keep on making the payments on a little home she'd bought. She wasn't very strong and had two little children.

Flint had been given six prize saddles along with his first prize winnings that year, of different shapes, styles and trimmings. He'd given two away to other cowboys and left the rest in saddle shops, as he'd done before, to be sold.

The new trophy he let the superintendent have to keep for him, telling him that it wasn't for champagne but if he ever filled it with such stuff and needed any help to empty it, to let him know.

That was the end for that year's contesting, and Flint let his saddle down from where it'd been hanging since he last left, and went to work on the rough ones on the range again. There'd be a few months of that on to the next year and time to light out to contesting again.

He always liked that big change from rodeo crowds and arenas, and after a day or so of cleaning out train soot, straightening things all around and putting on his comfortable and plain range clothes again, he as usual went to work on another rough string.

Flint wasn't much for sticking around towns, neither are most cowboys, and, as a rule, if he got his prize moneys and a train pulled out the evening of the last day of a contest, he was on that train and headed for other parts. He didn't care to go gallivanting around with the pretty girls such as tries to attract the cowboys, and there had to be some mighty good reasons before he'd go to parties and night clubs he was invited to; only sometimes, to please some of the townfolks he'd met and took a liking to, then again when he'd be sort of lonesome while waiting in some town for another rodeo to bust loose.

That's what bothered him most, the waiting, of sometimes a couple of weeks before a next big contest and he'd have to idle around in hotel lobbies and such places. The big contests often being far out from range countries, he wouldn't have enough time to get back "home" and stay long enough so it'd do him any good before he'd have to return, and the old 〰 outfit away out in the southern desert was plum out of the question to get back to between contests, from middle summer till late fall.

He spent one more winter with the rough ones there, took on a couple of small and close rodeos during that time and when the bigger ones begin to open up which led to the real big ones later on, Flint again felt in fine shape to take 'em on thru.

He took 'em on thru the West that summer and on up into Canada, all the best ones from the Pacific coast to the Atlantic, them along the Atlantic being the lastest ones in the year. And when he made his long way back west that year, to the ∿ outfit again, and come to figure out all the rodeos he'd been to and contested in, he seen where he'd took on many more than any year before. But even with that he also seen that he hadn't made as much money nor won as many first prizes as he had the three years past. But the money earnings was away second to what worried him most, which was that by all accounts he didn't do so good as before in his bronc riding.

He'd had fair judges as ever before, he thought, but now even tho that year's Association records showed him still high and at the top on points, he seen that with the half from points won the three or four years before, and with this year's record alone he'd be about fourth from the top. He also seen that, with all points of four years added, there was one contestant had crawled up pretty close to him. Hadn't been heard of only during the last two years but that cowboy had sure made some high and long strides as a contestant, and being the rodeos had got so numerous and been going so strong in that time, it didn't take long for a top contestant to get where he wanted to. Flint knew that contestant and also knew that he'd have to go some to keep him from getting above him on the following year.

Flint rode, roped and worked harder than ever before on the ∿ that winter and when he went into the thick of contesting again that summer he went at it mighty serious. But he didn't have that old and sure feeling of being champion any more, and that didn't help any.

That new and younger contestant was in near every rodeo Flint went to, specially the biggest ones, and more than gave him a ride for his money, so much so that at the last big rodeo that fall he was acclaimed champion bronc rider over Flint. But the new champion didn't get over Flint in roping and bull-dogging. Fact is he didn't try, the same as Flint hadn't tried in his first years of contesting.

And now, even tho Flint was replaced by another as world champion bronc rider, that didn't stop him from winning championships at other rodeos. Them championships would of course be only for each rodeo where he'd win and not as world's championships, not unless he got to his old stride again and beat that younger contestant.

Only a couple of years before, the younger and now new World champion didn't have a chance against Flint, and he still wouldn't of had much chance only Flint had got to his peak and the riding ability that was his and had made many an arena and contestant watch in wonder, was now on the downhill grade.

No human body is so that it can stand the rough treatment of hard bucking horses for many years. The amount and ages of them years average well with that of prize fighting, which is the next roughest contest on a man. And a bronc rider, if he stays at the game steady enough and keeps at the rough ones in between contests as Flint did, is thru before he's thirty. Thru at least for winning any fair-sized championships.

And, like with champion prize fighters, Flint didn't realize or figure that he was going down grade in his riding when the younger contestant got the championship over him. He still thought he'd rode as good as ever and that maybe he'd only been sort of unlucky in the drawing of his horses, they hadn't bucked good or hard enough to give him a chance to show the judges his riding ability which would bring him the points. "Can't win any points on a rocker," he'd say.

He put in another winter of tough and hard riding on the ~ outfit, and this time he didn't go out on the range and get in with the regular work there. Instead he done his riding into or close to the corrals at the main camp. This way he was topping off from ten to twelve head of the rough ones every day, where on the range he'd be changing only to two or three and along with the work to be done.

Flint sort of kept awatching himself as he rode horse after horse in the corral. He also went to the two close rodeos he'd been going to the last few winters, came out usual first in bronc riding, and by the time the bigger rodeos came on he felt sure he was as good as he'd ever been. He'd sure had plenty of good practice.

But even with all that practice and sure as he felt, the way the judges had him down on their books didn't jibe very well with that cowboy's expectations. He done good in the first and smaller rodeos and came out with first prize at a few of 'em, but the bigger rodeos that came on later had him kind of stumped, for it seemed that with them he got to feeling lucky to get up to second prize.

Then come a big twelve-day rodeo, with night performances to boot, and Flint thought that they was too long. He didn't stop to think of the millions in that city and vicinity, or that if the rodeo was to be held there for a month there wouldn't be over ten out of every hundred of the people would get to see it. Some of 'em wouldn't even know of it, others wouldn't care to see it in thinking it would only be cut and dried wild west stuff and would rather go to the opera or such, some business folks would be too busy to get away, and along with many others didn't know what it would be all about. Then there was of course many who'd liked to've gone in thru the big gates but didn't have the necessary money to buy a ticket.

But regardless of that, and out of them millions of people there'd be filled grandstands of appreciating spectators to witness the doings in the arena below. There'd of course be the usual few loud-mouthed smart alecs, but not like there is in any other contest or game, and at rodeos it's seen that such kind are put out, quick.

But Flint still couldn't get it into his head why such a long-winded rodeo. "Why, in this kind of city," he said, "a cowboy'll go broke with just paying entrance fees and feeding himself while waiting to be called for the events he's entered in, then there's rooms to pay for the nights, fares to here and back to home and then a feller also has to have a little fun when not needed in the arena and the contest closes up for the day, or night.

"There's only one good point to this marathon rodeo, and that's the prizes up for the winners. They're by twice the biggest I ever heard of, but then again you have to ride plenty oftener, and wait plenty time longer to get to them prizes and hit for home, if you've saved or made your face.

"But I'm here now and I'll have plenty of time to go after all I aim to get," was his final remark to that.

He entered in saddle and bareback bronc riding, steer riding, and, with steer roping, bull-dogging and other events he competed in, he managed to make good day moneys all around, won enough the first day to make up for what he had to pay on entrance fees, and he was competing on "velvet" from then on. He didn't have to touch none of his stored-away dinero, and even tho he helped some of the boys now and again, his daily winnings still kept him well up on velvet and accumulating.

But he more than had to compete to keep it that way, and as well as he done he still wasn't satisfied. He kept that to himself, but the matter was that he was again after another world championship, and the points hadn't stacked up much in his favor against "The Kid," as he called the feller who'd outrode him.

This kid, just past his twenties, at an age when he couldn't be hurt much, had never rode on the range. All the riding he'd ever done was inside sheltered stockyards. He smoked ready made cigarettes and chewed gum. If he'd got outside the town limits he'd got lost and bumped into a cow he might be looking for without ever seeing 'er.

But to his credit was that he had the natural born ability as a rider, and in the sales yards, where many horses was shipped in, auctioned, sold and shipped out, is where he'd got to learn to ride. In them yards is where he'd rode many horses of all kinds, many on inspection for different foreign government buyers, and he'd got so he could ride the toughest, which many of 'em was, and of no good on the range, but qualified for standards as to height, age, color and soundness for army requirements.

Such requirements being decided on, the inspection was simple; all the kid had to do was ride 'em past the officials for a short space of time, and whichever way they went out of the yard chutes, straight or crooked, didn't seem to matter. . . . Many of them horses, after they was boated acrost, turned out to be too tough for the officers and men that'd got their diplomas only thru riding academies, and so the horses, good ones, was condemned.

But the kid, and "this side," didn't worry about that. He kept on ariding and ariding until his ambitions got so high as to compete against such a cowboy as Flint.

He'd been stepping on that cowboy's spurs, crowded and won over on him, which all sure didn't set so well with Flint, and now, along with more "pistols" (younger riders) that'd sprouted up, he figured he'd be lucky if he seen any of the bronc money. His hope layed that he made the semi-finals and still would have a chance in the finals.

Satisfied with that, he kept up with the work he'd entered into in other events and got great satisfaction hearing his whaleline sing and felt it stretch as he piled his loop into big south going steers, and along as he stretched his rope that way and kept his hand on the slack to lay his steer, there was other tunes to the singing of that rope; with his hand on the strained line he'd got the feeling that with his biggest rodeo it would be the last one he'd be contesting into, and the while had peaceful visions of a green spot in the hills where he'd keep a few horses and his knitting bones would mend. (It was on account of them hurts he was later turned down when the World War broke out.)

But he wasn't going to quit a quitter at this last big rodeo, if it was to be his last. He contested harder than he ever had before, and consequences was he easy won first in steer roping, tied for first in bareback bronc riding, and rode good enough in the semi-final saddle bronc riding to make the finals. He made that in good shape, and next was the grand finals.

Now it was up to him and the kid and only a few other riders to compete and make it a wind up on the twelve day rodeo. That would be held for the last doings and when the champions would be declared and announced.

Flint had never felt nervous before, but now he was, and all thru irritation of the thought that a stockyard hand might win over an old butcher. He wouldn't of minded it so much if it'd been a good old regular cowboy outrode him, but with this yard hand doing that, it didn't at all go well with him.

He looked at the judges while he felt of his stirrup length on the ground by the saddling chutes, and seen by the poker faces of 'em that even tho they was for him, friends he knew, he wouldn't get no more points than should be credited to him. No favorites.

Flint didn't want to be no favorite or be classed as a judge's pet on decisions. He'd never allowed that, and the judges knew that an unfair decision in his favor would be slapped back in their faces, and maybe something else to boot.

He'd always won fair, in the toughest game any man can get into; the most cold-blooded and squarest game there is. . . . You can't "buy" a cowboy because his pride is more in his winnings than his earnings, and you sure can't "buy" a good bucking horse because they have their ambitions too, and the owner of 'em is just as proud to see that they're kept in shape to achieve their aim, as the cowboys are who ride 'em to get to theirs.

The kid was the second rider up, at the tenth hour of that evening, arc lights aflooding down on him and all over the arena. He made a wampus of a good ride, Flint thought, and now his only hope was that he'd drawed as good a bucking horse as the kid came out on. A couple more riders came out and done well but, to his judgment, not as good as the kid had. Then *Flint Spears* was announced as the next rider up.

Flint was in the saddle and ready and his name was no more than announced when there was a crash of timber, a five hundred pound chute gate was splintered, cowboys scattered, and out come something in horseflesh that wasn't a horse but more like what Satan had turned down, as too tough for him.

Men have been thirsty, men have been hungry, but no man ever craved so much for anything as what Flint set out on top of just then, grinning and scratching, so that the judges could hardly keep track of neither horse or rider. It was just fur aflying, earth ashaking, and when the whistle finally blowed, no pick-up man got time to get to Flint or his horse; he throwed his bucking rein up high in the air like as to say it was his grand-final ride, one that nobody could dispute, slid off the horse to land on his boot heels, let the horse buck on by, and with both hands up walked back to the chutes, the hankering look off his face and now again with the same smile he'd packed in his ten years of contesting.

At the eleventh hour that same evening, after all the riding was over and the rodeo come to an end, he was again presented a tall silver and gold trophy, a silver mounted saddle and pearl handle six-shooter and again acclaimed "*The World's All-Around Champion Cowboy.*"

*He throwed his bucking rein up high in the air
like as to say it was his grand-final ride.*

Again acclaimed "The World's All-Around Champion Cowboy."

XIV
THE LAST ROUND UP

I N A GOOD-SIZED two-roomed loghouse and by a big blazing fireplace there sat a cowboy, all in comfort. It was winter, a light skiff of snow which would melt away on the next day covered the ground. It was a cold night, for that country, but by the fireplace where a couple of good lengths of mesquite burned, it was all warm and cheerful and what any man could wish for.

On the wide mantel of the fireplace was tall shining trophies with gold mountings of bucking horses or steers' heads on 'em. On the log walls was enlarged photographs of more bucking horses, along with some of steer roping and bull-dogging, and more trophies such as bridles, belts and spurs ahanging between 'em here and there.

In one corner and on a rack was a fancy silver-mounted saddle, the last one this cowboy had won and would now keep, just to look at. Then in another corner, on a table which served as a desk and to keep magazines and such, was another big photograph. That one was in much contrast to the others of fast and unbelievable action of horses, cattle and cowboys. This picture was of the quiet, smiling and mighty pretty face of a girl. On the bottom of it was the writing "To Flint, with my love, Alberta." It was the only girl photograph in the house.

Flint had met Alberta near a year before at a small rodeo where all the contesting he'd entered into was steer roping. He'd met her thru her dad who he knew as being a cowman who had a ranch only two ridges over from where Flint now was. The girl didn't enter in any part of the contest. She was no contestant and Flint was somehow glad of that. But, as her dad said, she's sure a great little hand at home in the hills, in both roping and riding, and as Flint had been invited to visit 'em sometime, any time, which he did, he seen she was all her dad had said about her, and to Flint a considerable more.

Flint had never been attracted much by girls. But this time, well he'd went and built himself this neat log house which could easy be added onto and where he was enjoying such comfort that winter evening.

The building of that house had at first been against the advice of the ∾ superintendent where he'd come back to over a year before, after he'd won the championship. That feller had said it was foolish for him to go build a place when he could stay on the outfit for as long as he wanted to and work as he wanted to. But Flint had only grinned his thanks at that and said, "I want a place of my own. Besides, I need such a place to keep my things and put up my trophies."

"Yes," the superintendent had remarked at that, suspicious; "a feller gets tired of running around, no place to call home, and no smiling one to greet him open armed and . . ."

It was the same thing when he rode over to the 45 outfit to get the private saddle horses he'd left on the horse range there quite a few years before. That outfit wanted him there too.

And now, with the two big outfits, and being Flint was so set on having a place of his own, the main heads of them two outfits fearing he'd ride on out of the country and of losing him for good, had got together and decided on a good place for him, so he'd be right between 'em and a short ride from either outfit's main ranch. He could ride line for 'em if he wanted to and take on broncs or rough ones at extra wages. Each outfit would be able to furnish him with more than he could handle, and for as long as he wanted.

There was no buildings of any kind on the spot, but they would have the house, corrals and stable built for him to his taste and he could pay them for it with part of his wages, as he wished.

That all was a mighty good proposition, Flint thought. He'd always liked that country, much more so now that he'd met Alberta. He'd figured on going back home and staying and working with his folks but it was too fertile a country up there and his brother had wrote him not long before that it was getting pretty well farmed up. Then it was very cold up there of winters and deep snows for many months, where down here a few little skiffs of it which melted near as soon as it fell was about all there ever was, and there wasn't the expense nor work of feeding stock, which was something Flint sure considered as a great advantage.

He'd thought too of going up and working with Mark who by now was again able to ride, even tho only gentle ones. Mark had a good start and was doing well in the cow business again, so he wrote. His letters, the few he did write, sounded good and he kept arepeating in each one for Flint to come up and pitch camp with him for stay.

Flint had quite a bit of money saved up and could of went into partnership with him, adding on more cattle. But there again was another cold country, where stock often got snowbound and had to be fed all winter.

Now that he wasn't contesting no more he could run up and visit the folks once in a while or as often as he could, and that would have to do. He could also drop in on Mark for a few days.

Then he met Alberta and, well, that settled it, and that's how come he was enjoying all the comforts of life by his cheerful fireplace while a soft light flurry of snow was falling outside that evening.

That flurry would liven up the range some more, also the little meadow below the house. He'd had that plowed up and sowed into clover and blue grass for a good pasture. It did make a good pasture, near the year around, and there's where his horses run, with such good feed plum up to their eyes. A clear little mountain stream came by the house, which set by a grove of quakers and cottonwoods, was big enough to irrigate the little meadow during the long dry spells of that country, also leaving plenty to run on outside the fence to water all the stock that scope of range was carrying.

The house, stable corrals and all in the pretty location it was, then the lay of the country around was everything Flint could of dreamed of and wished to've owned, but he hadn't dreamed or even thought of such, not until the spring before, when he'd went to the little rodeo. Now he well realized he had just the place he would of dreamed of if he'd been so inclined before.

In the meadow, with Flint's own horses which now had got well on in age and he wasn't using no more, was always a half a dozen or

And there's where his horses run with such good feed plum up to their eyes.

so of either ∾ or 45 horses which he'd be breaking. These wasn't of the rough string kind, just plain good range horses, plenty wild and kinky, but hadn't got spoilt nor learned the tricks of how to fight as the old outlaws Flint had been used to on range and in rodeos.

That cowboy didn't want no more such horses, for being thru with contesting and needing no practice for that, he was now well satisfied in just breaking colts that'd never been handled before. These would be from three to six in ages and even tho some of 'em would rock pretty stiff, they was just play, and only stirred up a feller's appetite as compared to the buckers who knew how and cared for nothing else but that.

He would take on only about six colts at a time now, where it used to be ten or twelve. But he was having a mighty easy time with these few, and of course being he was now batching that took a little time too. Once in a while, when the colts would get a little hardened in, he'd take on line riding, and if he'd get a little lonesome or tired of his own cooking he'd take all the horses along and hit for the round-up camp of one or the other of the two outfits.

Once in a while he'd also cross the two mountain ridges for a visit with Alberta, but being he hadn't told of his intentions and that he always went there with the excuse he was looking for cattle or horses that'd strayed away, the old folks would be present to chat during about half of his visiting time.

Then again, being it was a good day's ride from his place to the girl's, her folks would always insist on his staying over night. That made him feel as a sort of grub-line rider and there was no way he could repay. So, on that account, he didn't go to visiting there as much as he'd liked to, not near as much. But some day he was going to get up enough courage and tell the old folks that he was coming out there to do some real courting.

But that'd have to wait yet, for, by rights he'd ought to stock up his surrounding range with cattle and make it all real homey-like. He had plenty of money to buy a good little bunch with and still have some left for other things. Besides he was making good enough money at breaking these colts to keep things going. He'd turn a fairly well broke bunch of 'em over every two or three weeks, then he'd get a fresh bunch, and at eight to ten dollars per head for breaking each bunch, that wasn't bad. Besides he could go on with that work and right along with riding after his cattle when he'd get 'em. He didn't want to keep up this horse breaking business for long anyway, just long enough so he'd have enough cattle to make him and two or six a good living along with being able to afford some luxeries, plenty of shelter and comfort.

He thought of wanting to get into more cattle from the start, go to contesting again, save more money and ride for the big stakes to win and so he could do that. He'd thought of that for quite some time, and finally, that night while the soft snow was falling outside and he was inside by the fireplace he got to figuring strong on the idea. He got up from his chair, went to his desk table and rummaging around there got a little vest pocket book. In it was names, addresses, figures, brands and a sort of a record of all the rodeos and moneys he'd won the past ten years or so, of his contesting.

With a pad and pencil he added up how much he'd made each year. The first year, he'd won five hundred, but it went up fast a couple of years after that, and then as he kept on adding up each year, he was surprised that it went up to where one year he made over ten thousand dollars, the biggest money any champion cowboy had ever made contesting, and the biggest Flint had made in any other year, even tho being the all-around champion he was.

And to go against that year's big earnings he remembered he'd contested mighty hard. He also remembered that he'd spent quite a considerable sum at that same time. Traveling on trains from one contest to another, waiting at hotels for long spells between contests, then more hotels during them, all took plenty of money, more than he'd imagined, and then there was the entrance fees, expensive clothes to keep him looking neat and which would be plum useless on the range, doing his share at high priced hifaluting parties that was sometimes put on, paying other cowboys' entrance fees, helping some that got stranded, some hurt, and others in hospitals was all part of what every contestant had to put up with if he was a sure enough cowboy.

Flint had partly jotted down some of his expenses during that year's big winnings, and even tho some of 'em was missing, he seen where out of that ten thousand he'd made, he didn't come clear with over four thousand.

It's hard to do any stingeing in the rodeo contesting game, as hard as the game is itself. None come out of it anywheres near rich, only in experiences, cuts, shattered bones and bruises.

Flint wasn't for extravagant spending in any way but there wasn't many years of his contesting when he could come out in the clear with two thousand, and figuring that out as he was doing on his tablet that evening, he was now already doing near as well. Then with a good bunch of cattle he could double that without the grind of hard contesting nor the soot of long traveling.

As he summed that all up he soon gave up the idea of going contesting again. Then after considering some more on the subject, he got to thinking and realizing that he wasn't the Flint Spears of some years ago. He of course had mended up and felt as good as new, would for as long as any wiry human. But there's something to this steady contesting game that does something to a feller, and the best of 'em can last just so long.

Another thing Flint got to considering was that he'd come out slick and clean with title of World Champion All-Around Cowboy at the last and big twelve-day rodeo he'd contested in. That was a great honor, mighty tough to get up to. It was a record he could always be proud of, and he come to decide he'd better let things rest that way. He wouldn't want to mar that now with any second or third moneys, which is what he figured he'd soon come to, for he was true enough with himself to realize that as a bronc rider he'd passed the high marks.

Only one thing he'd do now, as far as contesting was concerned, would be to show up at some of the close rodeos, not over a couple of hundred miles away, and maybe enter only in steer roping, as he'd done a few times the summer before. He'd went more to visit with the boys he'd contested with and the fun in general than to win anything.

With his widespread reputation as champion he was asked to contest in many events at every rodeo he went to. Then, when it was heard that he'd quit contesting there was calls for him to act as judge at the little, big and biggest rodeos, scattering from coast to coast and border to border. Some of 'em offered mighty good fees, but Flint wasn't interested. He was afraid he might not be fair, for he could only see his own way of riding and that would make it sort of tough on the cowboys if they didn't qualify to that standard.

He stayed up late that night, figuring all these things out, and now, with pad and pencil and all making it clear to him, he decided for good and all time to leave the contesting alone and do just as he had the past year, visit at a few of the rodeos and spread on with what he now had, his home and plans for the happy future he seen ahead right there.

He felt relieved and happy at that conclusion, and now he got up, put away the little book, looked again at the smiling face on the table desk there, blowed out the lamp, and by the glow of the warm light from the fireplace flickering against the ceiling he crawled into his bed and went to sleep, still the *Champion All-Around Cowboy.*

Still the Champion All-Around Cowboy

The pictures on the following pages were all made from photographs taken at rodeos held at different times in various parts of the country. They were selected by the author from many others as being typical of the experiences of Flint Spears and other cowboy contestants in the rodeo.

The rules printed opposite the first six pictures are those of the Rodeo Association and the ones governing the particular contest shown in the picture facing them.

EVENT NUMBER ONE

COWBOYS' BAREBACK BRONK RIDING CONTEST
FOR THE CHAMPIONSHIP OF THE WORLD

[Entrance Fee—$15.00]

13 Day Moneys (26 Performances)—First, $75.00
Second, $50.00; Third, $30.00; Fourth, $20.00

Contestant making highest average will be awarded
WORLD'S CHAMPIONSHIP TITLE AND TROPHY

CONDITIONS

The cowboy who wins First Place at each performance must be ready and willing to ride into the arena and be announced before the close of the performance, or he will receive no marking for that ride.

Riders must draw for mounts daily. Any rider turning down a horse or refusing to ride when called upon shall be disqualified and not allowed to ride that day or any day following in this event, and also shall forfeit his entrance fee.

This is a one-hand contest. Riders must ride with regulation surcingle, which will be furnished by the Management. Riders must ride with one hand on the surcingle and the other in the air and must leave the chute with both spurs in shoulders and continuously scratch the horse until the sound of the whistle.

—RODEO RULES

COWGIRLS' BRONK RIDING CONTEST FOR THE CHAMPIONSHIP OF THE WORLD

[Entrance Fee—$15.00]

13 Day Moneys (26 Performances)—First, $75.00
Second, $50.00; Third, $30.00; Fourth, $20.00

Final Moneys: First, $200.00 and
WORLD'S CHAMPIONSHIP TITLE AND TROPHY
Second, $150.00 and Third, $100.00 and Fourth, $50.00

*The amount of day money will be paid according to the
number of performances required to complete one go-around.*

CONDITIONS

Any rider turning down horse, or refusing to ride when called upon, shall be disqualified and not allowed to ride for day money that day or any day following in this event, and shall also forfeit her entrance fee.

The highest total markings on all horses wins final money.

This will be a hobble stirrup contest and no extra points will be allowed for riding slick.

All riders to use committee saddles and two reins.

Committee saddles will be furnished by the management.

All horses will be saddled by the saddle judge.

The cowgirl who wins First at each performance must be ready and willing to ride into the arena and be announced before the close of each performance.

Positively no re-rides allowed unless horse falls before disqualification.

Any of the following offences disqualify rider:
    Not being ready when called upon to ride
    Changing hand on reins or losing rein
    Being bucked off
    Pulling leather
    Hitting horse with hat or hand
    Losing stirrup.

—RODEO RULES

One of these steers can't be stopped with words and won't come home of evenings—it takes good strong hemp fastened to a good horse to make 'em face you, and then the battle is still not over.

EVENT NUMBER THREE

COWBOYS' CALF ROPING CONTEST FOR THE CHAMPIONSHIP OF THE WORLD

[Entrance Fee—$100.00]

13 Day Moneys (26 Performances)—First, $125.00
Second, $100.00; Third, $90.00; Fourth, $80.00; Fifth, $70.00

Final Moneys: First, $350.00 and 20% of total entrance fees
and WORLD'S CHAMPIONSHIP TITLE AND TROPHY
Second, $250.00 and 15% of total entrance fees; Third, $200.00 and
10% of total entrance fees; Fourth, $120.00 and 5% of total entrance fees

CONDITIONS

There shall be three timekeepers, a tie judge, a foul line judge and one starter. All calves to be penned and any objectionable calves cut out. Calves will be given dead line start in accordance with Arena conditions, and when calf crosses dead line he is roper's calf, regardless of what happens. TEN SECONDS FINE FOR ROPER'S MOUNT BEING OVER FOUL LINE WHEN STARTER'S FLAG DROPS.

This is a CATCH-AS-CATCH-CAN CONTEST, but a catch must be made with the rope that will hold calf until the roper gets to him. Roper must adjust rope and reins in a manner to prevent his horse busting calf.

Roper must dismount and go down rope and throw calf by hand. Should calf be down when roper gets to him, he must be let up on his feet and thrown by hand. Must cross any three feet and tie so as to hold calf until passed upon by the tie judge. Tie to be passed upon by the judge, and roper will not be allowed to touch calf in any manner after signalling for time, until judgment of the tie has been pronounced by tie judge. Calf will be left tied down as long as deemed necessary by judge to ascertain if tie is complete.

Each roper must have neck rein or strap around horse's neck, adjusted to positively prevent dragging of calf.

All calves will be numbered and drawn for. Roper will be disqualified for trailing calf down.

A 10 seconds fine will be added if roper or horse busts calf.

Each roper will be allowed only two loops but he must throw both loops or catch calf before retiring from the arena.

If roper's horse drags calf over 12 inches, he will be fined 10 seconds.

A time limit of 75 seconds will be placed on calf roper and if roper has not completed his catch and tie when the 75 seconds have expired, he will be signalled to retire from the arena and given no time.

The cowboy who wins First at each performance must be ready and willing to ride into the arena and be announced or he shall receive no time.

The management reserves the right to change or add to the above rules if necessary to meet local conditions.

—RODEO RULES

COWBOYS' BRONK RIDING CONTEST FOR
THE CHAMPIONSHIP OF THE WORLD

[Entrance Fee—$30.00]

13 Day Moneys (26 Performances)—First, $100.00; Second, $85.00; Third, $75.00
Fourth, $65.00; Fifth, $55.00; Sixth, $45.00; Seventh, $35.00; Eighth, $25.00

The cowboy winning the highest markings on all mounts will be awarded the
WORLD'S CHAMPIONSHIP TROPHY AND TITLE

CONDITIONS

The cowboy who wins First at each performance must be ready and willing to ride into the arena and be announced before the close of the performance or he will receive no markings on that ride.

The management will furnish saddle judges that will pass on all equipment and supervise the saddling and cinching of all horses.

Each horse will be marked on his shoulders where the saddle must set.

Any rider turning down horse, or refusing to ride when called upon, shall be disqualified and not allowed to ride for day money that day or any day following in this event, and shall also forfeit his entrance fee.

The judges will draw mounts for riders daily. Riders must ride as often as judges may require.

Hamley Committee saddles will be furnished by the management, and no private saddles will be allowed in this contest. If a saddle is not cinched tight enough and comes off, the rider shall be given a re-ride on the same horse. The Management will appoint one man to flank all horses.

The Management will furnish a saddle judge who will pass on all equipment and saddling of every horse before leaving chute.

Rider will be disqualified on judges' decision if rider has purposely cheated the horse to keep him from doing his best. Riding to be done with plain halter and one rein, which shall be furnished by the Management. Rider will not be allowed to use his own reins. No knots or wraps around the hand allowed, no tape on stirrup or rein. Pulling horse's head shall be counted against rider. Rein must come up on the same side of horse's neck as the hand the rider rides with. Rider must hold rein at least six inches above horse's neck while bucking. Horses to be saddled in the chute or Arena as the Management may decide. Rider must leave starting place with both feet in the stirrups, with toes turned out and both spur rowels moving against the horse's shoulder. Must scratch front for the first five jumps, then scratch high behind, then both ways until the whistle is blown. Rider must ride with one hand free and not change hands on rein. Chaps, spurs, saddle, rein and boots to be passed upon by the judges.

Should rider ride according to rules and horse fails to buck, he shall be given another horse. Rider will be given a re-ride on same horse if an accident should happen, if the judges consider it necessary in order to judge either horse or rider.

Should the rider ride according to rules and horse falls before whistle is blown, the judges shall order horse picked up and rider will be given a re-ride on same horse.

Each rider must adjust stirrups before saddling. No locked spur rowels allowed.

Management reserves the right to change rules if necessary to meet local conditions on approval of judges.

Any of the following offences disqualifies rider:

Losing stirrup
Changing hands on rein or losing rein
Being bucked off
Coasting with feet against horse's shoulder
Not scratching horse with spur rowels
Wrapping reins around hand
Pulling leather
Hitting horse with hat or hand
Failing to leave starting place with spur rowels against horse's shoulder
Cutting or defacing saddles and equipment,
Not being ready when called upon to ride.

—RODEO RULES

COWBOYS' STEER WRESTLING CONTEST FOR
THE CHAMPIONSHIP OF THE WORLD

[Entrance Fee—$100.00]

13 Day Moneys (26 Performances)—First, $125.00
Second, $100.00; Third, $90.00; Fourth, $80.00; Fifth, $70.00

Final Moneys: First, $350.00 and 20% of total entrance fees and
WORLD'S CHAMPIONSHIP TITLE AND TROPHY
Second, $250.00 and 15% of total entrance fees; Third, $200.00 and
10% of total entrance fees; Fourth, $120.00 and 5% of total entrance fees.

CONDITIONS

The cowboy who makes the fastest time at each performance must be ready and willing to ride into the arena and be announced before the close of each performance or he will receive no time on that particular steer.

Each wrestler is required to make at least one catch from his horse and if he does not make an honest effort to stop or throw steer, he must mount his horse and catch steer again.

This rule will be determined and judged by the field judge.

If field judge requests wrestler to make a second catch and the wrestler refuses, he will then be disqualified.

Steers will be numbered and drawn for, and any wrestler GUILTY OF TAMPERING WITH STEERS, CHUTE OR NUMBERS WILL BE DISQUALIFIED.

Wrestler and hazer will be allowed to leave the chute with steer, wrestler's mount and steer may be Lap-and-Tap when crossing dead line, but wrestler must not have hand on steer or leap before crossing dead line, penalty not less than 15 seconds.

Steer belongs to wrestler when he crosses dead line regardless of what happens. All steers must be thrown by hand. This is a twist-down contest—wrestler must stop steer and twist him down. If steer is accidentally knocked down, he must be let up on all four feet and thrown again, and should steer start running after once being stopped and then be thrown by wrestler putting horns against the ground, then steer must be let up again and twisted down.

Wrestler must throw steer, and signal judges with one hand for time. Steer will be considered down when he is lying flat on his side, all feet out and head straight. Should wrestler let steer up before being told to do so by field judge, 30 seconds will be added to his time.

Should wrestler loosen or knock off horn he shall receive NO TIME on steer. Wrestler must be ready and take steer in his turn, or ten seconds will be added to his time.

Best total time on all steers wins final money.

A time limit of two minutes will be placed on wrestling, and if a wrestler has caught his steer but not been able to throw him when the two minutes have expired he will be signaled to retire from the Arena and given no time.

After the wrestler has caught his steer, hazer must retire at direction of field judge. In event wrestler jumps and misses his steer, he will be allowed only the aid of his hazer in catching and remounting his horse.

Fifteen seconds will be added to wrestler's time if his hazer helps in any way to keep steer from running with wrestler after leap is made, such as riding in front of steer.

Wrestler who, in the opinion of the judges, abuses the steer in any manner, will be disqualified. WRESTLER MUST CATCH STEER FROM HORSE.

Any steer wrestler failing to take steer in turn or refusing to try to throw steer will be disqualified from this and any other event in which he is entered.

The Management reserves the right to change or add to the above rules if necessary to meet local conditions.

—RODEO RULES

EVENT NUMBER SIX

COWBOYS' STEER RIDING CONTEST FOR THE CHAMPIONSHIP OF THE WORLD

[Entrance Fee—$15.00]

13 Day Moneys (26 Performances)—First, $80.00
Second, $60.00; Third, $40.00; Fourth, $30.00 and Fifth, $20.00

Contestant making the highest markings on all mounts will be awarded WORLD'S CHAMPIONSHIP TITLE AND TROPHY.

CONDITIONS

The cowboy who wins first at each performance must be ready and willing to ride into the arena and be announced before the close of each performance or he will receive no markings on that mount.

Any rider who does not make an honest attempt to ride his steer, will be disqualified in this event and all other events in which he is entered.

Steers to be numbered and drawn for daily. Any rider turning down a steer or refusing to ride when called upon shall be disqualified and not allowed to ride for day money that day or any other day following in this event.

This is a one-hand contest. Riders must leave chute with both spurs against steer's neck and scratch him all the time until sound of whistle, which is the signal to dismount.

—RODEO RULES

STAGE COACH RACE

Where most always the coaches tangle or crash, mixing up teams, coaches, drivers and all in a great mess.

CHUCK WAGON RACE

This is as bad as the stage coach race only sometimes worse. The cowboys in the wagons often have to scramble plenty fast to keep out from under some overturning wagon and sometimes only one team comes in, after breaking loose from the scramble.

TRICK ROPING

It's hard enough to do good roping while sitting in the saddle or from the ground, but to do it standing in the saddle is one feat you can't get by just talking or reading about it.

EASY FOR HIM

Here's another good roping feat, five horses caught by the front feet at once. That's about like getting your mouth around a double five deck sandwich.

TRICK RIDING

With years of hard practice you can do this, if you don't eat too much and keep up the practice. It'll keep you in shape.

SINGLE STEER ROPING

Heavy landing for the steer—notice four feet and whole
steer up—that steer was plenty wild and wanted to get
away—That makes good roping and the rope sings.

A HARD LANDING

Poor feller, away up there. It looks like it's going to be a hard landing—But he didn't land the first time, for the bull, watching for him to come down after the toss up, *gently* caught him in his horns and tossed him up again.

Ready for the kill but not for the bull. After cowboys drove the bull away this toreador from Mexico took a ride to the hospital.

Find the cowboy—He's well under a lot of wild horse flesh.

GOOD PONY AND GOOD COWBOY

The horse is a "final" horse and the
cowboy rode to win the "finals."

Final horses are the picked worst and the
cowboy who wins on 'em is sure to be the best.

© Doubleday

This cowboy had no intentions of riding backwards nor so high but the gray bucker, with hard back-twists and jolts would set any rider to thinking the earth was up and the stars was down. The mild look on the gray's head is just plain satisfaction in getting his man—

THROWED BUCKING REIN AND STIRRUPS AWAY

This cowboy didn't want to get in the rumble seat of his saddle but a bronc don't care what his rider wants, it's what he wants and that's to give his rider a good tossing and then get out from under him.

But it's hard telling, this cowboy might still get back in the saddle—

This pony, not satisfied with getting his man down, is going after him with good intentions of finishing him and pounding him into the ground. (Like old Smoky when he was named the cougar.)

NO CHANCE FOR A COWBOY HERE

When a bucking horse gets so ambitious, goes high and doesn't land on his feet (notice foot still in the stirrup) the cowboy is out of luck.

Will James was born Joseph Ernest Nephtali Dufault in the province of Quebec on June 6, 1892. He left home as a teenager to live out his dream of becoming a cowboy in the American West. James went on to write and illustrate twenty-four books and numerous magazine articles about horses, cowboying, and the West. His works soon captured the imagination of the public. He died in 1942, at the age of fifty.

We encourage you to patronize your local bookstore. Most stores will order any title that they do not stock. You may also order directly from Mountain Press using the order form provided below or by calling our toll-free number and using your MasterCard or VISA. We will gladly send you a complete catalog upon request.

Other fine Will James Titles:

_____	Cowboys North and South	14.00/paper	25.00/cloth
_____	The Drifting Cowboy	14.00/paper	25.00/cloth
_____	Smoky, the Cowhorse	16.00/paper	36.00/cloth
_____	Cow Country	14.00/paper	25.00/cloth
_____	Sand	16.00/paper	30.00/cloth
_____	Lone Cowboy	16.00/paper	30.00/cloth
_____	Sun Up	16.00/paper	30.00/cloth
_____	Big-Enough	16.00/paper	30.00/cloth
_____	Uncle Bill	14.00/paper	26.00/cloth
_____	All in the Day's Riding	16.00/paper	30.00/cloth
_____	The Three Mustangeers	15.00/paper	30.00/cloth
_____	Home Ranch	16.00/paper	30.00/cloth
_____	Young Cowboy		15.00/cloth
_____	In the Saddle with Uncle Bill	14.00/paper	26.00/cloth
_____	Scorpion, A Good Bad Horse	15.00/paper	30.00/cloth
_____	Cowboy in the Making		15.00/cloth
_____	Flint Spears, Cowboy Rodeo Contestant	15.00/paper	30.00/cloth
_____	Ride for the High Points: _The Real Story of Will James_ (Jim Bramlett)	20.00/paper	
_____	The Will James Books: _A Descriptive Bibliography for Enthusiasts and Collectors_ (Don Frazier)	18.00/paper	

Please include $3.00 per order to cover postage and handling.

Please send the books marked above. I have enclosed $ _____

Name _____

Address _____

City/State/Zip _____

☐ Payment enclosed (check or money order in U.S. funds)

Bill my: ☐ VISA ☐ MasterCard Expiration Date: _____

Card No _____

Signature _____

MOUNTAIN PRESS PUBLISHING COMPANY
P. O. Box 2399 • Missoula, MT 59806
Order Toll-Free **1-800-234-5308** • _Have your MasterCard or VISA ready_
e-mail: mtnpress@montana.com • website: www.mountainpresspublish.com